MALCOLM HOLLINGDRAKE

Book Fourteen in the Harrogate Crime Series

Also by Malcolm Hollingdrake

Bridging the Gulf

Shadows from the Past
Short Stories for Short Journeys

The Harrogate Crime Series

Only the Dead

Hell's Gate

Flesh Evidence

Game Point

Dying Art

Crossed Out

The Third Breath

Treble Clef

Threadbare

Fragments

Uncertainty of Reason

The Damascene Moment

Trapped Secrets

The Merseyside Series – Published by Hobeck Books

Catch as Catch Can

Syn

Edge of the Land

Short Story

'A piece of Paper that Changed a Life'

Published in the charity anthology, *Everyday Kindness*
Edited by L. J. Ross.

Dedicated to

Sue Martin

A dear friend

Regret is a form of punishment itself.

Nouman Ali Khan

Chapter 1

The fine flurries of snow were more of an annoyance than a joyous, late, festive encore. The white, fine blanket that covered the steep sides of the valley leading away from Blubberhouses up Kex Gill towards Ravens Peak, did make a postcard view from within the warmth of the car. Its offering did not, however, fill DI David Owen with any enthusiasm for the task ahead. The human remains had been discovered during the road building that had started months earlier to bring traffic away from the problematic and snaking A59. The route had been there for centuries and was now, owing to the sheer weight and number of vehicles using the road, prone to landslip.

Even though there was a covering of snow, the new scar created by the construction was as clear to see as was the extensive area of activity close to and around the discovery site. That too was now cordoned. The brightly coloured forensic tents, like the blue scars made by carbon dust that filled the cuts and scratches seen on many a miner, sat on what appeared to be a snowy white skin. There were three in total.

DI David Owen slipped on a pair of wellington boots

before drawing his scarf tightly around his neck as he began trudging over the semi-frozen ground. The deep corrugations of mud created by the heavy construction traffic were in places connected by a filigree of ice, making negotiating the short distance towards the police tape a struggle. There was no clear and defined route as the discovery, although treated as a crime scene, did not have the same priority on preserving surface and peripheral evidence. It was clear that the recently found remains had been in the ground for quite some time.

"There's more than one body." The Crime Scene Manager spoke between blowing onto her hands whilst trying to keep the electronic tablet tucked beneath her arm. "You might say we were lucky to discover them but maybe not as you stand here. There are warmer places I might choose. A bulldozer, if that's what that great leviathan is still called, seemingly tried to destroy everything within its path." She nodded towards the yellow ground-moving vehicle parked some distance away. "Making the true location of the original burial site difficult to locate." She pointed to the furthest tent and back. There was a look of uncertainty on Owen's face.

"How many?"

"Sorry, two. We have three femurs. We'll be looking for the missing one."

"Assuming one wasn't a pirate." Owen grinned but his tasteless comment was quickly dismissed. Her look spoke a thousand words.

"No full skulls at present but the forensic archaeologists are busy within the various tents. We have a Dr Green here, too, he's a forensic anthropologist." She blew on her hands once again and added the time of Owen's arrival to the electronic tablet.

Owen nodded as he thrust his hands deeper into his overcoat pockets. He had requested Dr Green's attendance. "We can only hope, especially as the burial site's been extensively bulldozed. Knowing if they've been buried a year or many, many years is key but until we have that information, we have a potential murder or murders." Owen turned and looked across the closed road towards the church of St Andrew on the far side. "I doubt they came from there. There's no graveyard if I remember."

"There's not. This bypass isn't due to open for a further twelve months but the A59 is scheduled to reopen as soon it's reinforced and secured."

"We found a body up there a while back, stuffed in a plastic tube can you believe." Owen pointed and his finger wavered in the general direction towards the upper area of the twisting road.

"Could these be—" She did not finish as Owen was already shaking his head.

"Not unless they were found inside plastic pipes."

"Pipes? No."

Owen wanted to ask if they were sure the remains were human and not animal but thought better of it. He bobbed below the tape and followed the footprints within the snow, ice and mud. Dr Green appeared outside a large tent as Owen approached. They had not met before. Owen raised a hand. Green smiled and thrust his latex gloved hands beneath his arm pits.

"DI David Owen. Dr Green?"

He nodded and smiled. "Bloody cold, Detective

Inspector. Come into my parlour. We cannot create any more chaos on this site and you might find it a bit warmer."

Disappointingly, the inside seemed only marginally better but it removed the wind chill. Much of the soil had been rearranged as numerous items they had discovered had been bagged and signed. A number of plastic boxes were neatly numbered and stacked. Photographs were still being taken of the remaining bones and bone fragments in situ. Owen was rather taken aback by Green's appearance. The flat cap reminded him of those worn in the television series, *Peaky Blinders,* a bow tie was just visible at his neck and the salt and pepper goatee beard seemed to give him a genteel if not incongruous look. The round, tortoiseshell glasses suggested the appearance of a vicar or solicitor. He was not what Owen expected for a scientist.

"Bit of a mess as everything's been churned but the pathologist and myself will be able to make more sense of it all once the remains are back. My immediate estimate, and I stress that's all it can be at this stage, is that they've been in the ground for approximately forty years."

From his screwed-up expression Owen got the idea it was more of a guess.

"We also have traces of fabric, as you might be able to see in this bag. Once we've retrieved all we can we shall detect for metal. That process may find surgery pins, jewellery, metal buttons or badges. These can often be more valuable in ascertaining their identity. The teeth, of course are always valuable."

Owen looked at the bone remnants, the deep brown staining gave them the appearance of wood. "I'm amazed anyone could identify them as bones. They look like bits of rotting branches."

"It's funny you should say that as we've sieved through numerous roots and branches. Before our work began, this area was a thicket of well-established trees and saplings. Although the trees were cleared you can imagine the root systems that had to be removed, hence that machine over there. To answer your question, we were lucky that one of the workers found the lower jaw bone, immediately knew what they were looking at and raised the alarm."

"Could it not have been from a sheep or animal?" Owen's question lacked conviction.

"Animals don't have fillings, Detective Inspector." Dr Green raised his eyebrows; they too were flecked with grey. "It's a sensible question as we've discovered the remains of a sheep mixed with the bones."

"What about the fleece?" Owen frowned.

Green smiled at the Inspector's naivety. "Biodegradable, they use them for compost. May last up to two years depending on the conditions, like all things that rot, but there may be a reason we found it there. It will take us another day to clear this area. We have pinpointed the approximate starting point from where the top soil was removed so we're fairly certain of the location the bodies were initially interred and the subsequent spread of that soil. It's a case of working back. Once we have the bones secured, we can attempt to put them together, do various tests and scans and try to identify them. If lucky, we'll be able to link them with missing persons. However, it's amazing how people can simply go missing and nobody seems to know they've gone."

"Police in London were searching the Thames for the

body of one man and found five." Owen shook his head as if in disbelief. "Five can you believe?"

"A bit like buses!" Green muttered, whilst moving the ground with his foot.

Owen grinned.

"Sorry, bad taste. We've had so many people entering the country illegally, some in wagons and now many in boats. Nobody knows they are here or who they are and so if they go missing, nobody goes looking for them. I'm surprised they only found five. Many of these illegals put themselves immediately in harm's way, I'm afraid."

Owen was only too aware of the growing social issues created by people trafficking. To Owen it was the scourge of society but he did not want to express his opinion on such a controversial issue at this stage. "So, if this area were wooded between here and the main road, it would be easy to dispose of a body or two without being seen. I believe the only house is located beyond the hedge a few hundred feet away."

Green pointed towards the house. "Don't forget there's also a stream. Now, part of that water course has been run below ground to come up just beyond Hall Lane. From there it's untouched and runs into Swinsty Reservoir and that was built and finished in 1887 so one of the CSI informed me. You'd be wise looking for aerial photographs of the area depending on what we discover from our tests. What it was like fifty years ago is just before my time and I'm sure yours, Detective Inspector. Remember also, the bodies might not have been placed here at the same time. If it has proved successful on one occasion, it might be the ideal location for the perfect murder or murders." Green rubbed his hands together. "Sorry to be Job's comforter."

Owen frowned, uncertain as to whom Job might be, before thanking Dr Green. He slipped out of the tent. Immediately a high-pitched screeching call startled him; it came from somewhere high above in the grey sky. Scanning briefly, he found the source, observing the broad wings of a large, brown bird he assumed to be a buzzard, soaring majestically in ever increasing circles. It brought to mind a vulture for some bizarre reason but it also raised a smile.

***

The press release detailing the discoveries had received the usual flurry of calls in response. The majority could be identified as cranks but each still needed to be processed and checked. Owen dipped his fingers into the mug positioned on the edge of his desk and withdrew an Uncle Joe's Mint Ball. The ambience of the police station always seemed so depressing just into the New Year. Whatever effort had been made to bring in the spirit of Christmas had equally been present in its swift removal. If you looked into the upper corners of the room, the occasional Sellotaped fragment of hastily torn down tinsel was still in evidence. His offering, a solitary snow globe displaying York Minster, had long been relegated to the bottom drawer until the following year.

The desk calendar displayed January 5th. Tomorrow, DCI Cyril Bennett would return. It was unusual for him to have spent such a long spell away and Owen for one would be happy to see his return.

Chapter 2

West Park, the one-way road running through the main area of Harrogate, edged the Stray to one side. The many skeletal winter trees, spread evenly along the road's edge, allowed a clear view to the far side of the broad green space. There, at the furthest point sat the apartment blocks, concrete sixties developments, now weathered, mellowed and softened and yet still looking incongruous in this half-light. The pathway scars running at angles across the Stray, were still busy with the dark, shadowy figures of dog walkers and commuters. Owing to the sun being hidden for most of the day by the grey mantle of cloud, a light dusting of snow still lingered in places but was now tinged with an orange bloom cast by the many street lights.

The hotel room, although small, was warm. Looking down at the coffee table, positioned in front of the window, were the playing cards, spread carefully in the form of a circle. Strangely, to the lone figure, it seemed appropriate that the game, the game that was always played in these circumstances, when time hung like treacle, was Solitaire.

The sound of a car's horn necessitated another brief glance out of the windows. The view had quickly changed.

Small, coloured fairy lights decorating the peripheral row of trees sparkled more brightly now, set against the black of the Stray. Those two views, in what seemed like only moments apart, were yin and yang; that simple thought brought a smile; it was a favourite symbol. *Why was yin dark, negative and feminine whilst yang was light, positive and masculine?* The thought lingered fleetingly. For some reason the masculine and feminine labels seemed to be unsatisfactory, unless, of course, you had witnessed a specific kind of cruelty. A hand quickly turned another card. For the solitary figure, the night had only just begun, a night that had been planned for quite some time. On this occasion, the dark could only be a positive, irrespective of what else might change within the pattern of the universe; that would be anyone's guess. Would people know why? Would they even care? Time, it had been decided, would be the healer as well as the harbinger of retribution and although it was a simple yet cruel cure, there was uncertainty as to whether it would bring a return to life's balance, but that was a necessary risk.

***

It was not that the day had come early, it was more that sleep had been denied. The darkness beyond the venetian blinds was still thick and claustrophobic; even with the street lights' glow it failed to penetrate the room to any degree to make a difference. Fine, needle-like sharp daggers of yellow were all that pierced the gloom. There was an annoying restlessness, an inability to find sleep, a sleep that he knew should recharge and bring inner rest.

Julie's low, rhythmic breathing, mixed with the warmth and the dark, should have been a soporific cocktail, the antidote to his insomnia, but it proved not to be. Cyril had drifted in and out of consciousness but those times had seemed fleeting and momentary, shallow. On reflection, these nights always followed the same pattern after a time away from work ... a time he had been reluctant to take off. Yet once away, even though he failed to admit it, he had enjoyed the respite, the normality of time and place. It was precious time to share with Julie and although these breaks were valued, he was often pleased to see them draw to an end – *You could have too much of a good thing*, he would often say to justify his feelings, but often no one was listening.

Now, the thought of work nagged like the stubborn, incessant chill of the breeze that he felt as it was often forced against his face during his daily walks on the winter Stray. He was now at the metaphorical fulcrum between play and work, it was a delicate balance and his feelings were mixed. Like this very moment of indecision, he deliberated if it were too early to rise when it seemed too late to search for sleep.

Leaning towards the bedside cabinet he collected his watch, the blue-green lume of the numerals on the face glowed enough to confirm it to be too early. He lay back and stared into the pitchy blackness and wondered what the New Year would bring. He felt a tingle of excitement course through him. He slid from the bed before popping on a dressing gown and at the same time moved quietly to the kitchen. Flicking on the under-cupboard lights, the room became flooded with a subtle, warm glow.

Tea, he needed tea. With cup and saucer in hand he

settled to enjoy the brew. For some reason he felt the New Year was going to be one of the best, a new chapter, positive and successful. For the first time for as long as he could remember, he felt at peace with himself, his past, his life and his career. He knew that he had laid some ghosts to rest and to his surprise, no new ones had come haunting ... not yet at least!

His suit was pressed. As he brushed the jacket's shoulders and collar, he felt a surge of exhilaration to be returning to work. Removing the shoe trees he checked the leather's shine. He was happy. All was shipshape. As he approached the front door his hand moved instinctively around his body. "Spectacles, testicles, wallet and watch." He was gone.

***

Betty Cole's morning was not about to begin. She lay face up on the floor where she had remained since her world had gone silent and dark. Part of the broken green bottle was positioned near her head; the base appeared like a round, verdant island set within a congealing, blood red sea. The smooth and rounded inner punt enveloped by the jagged, broken edges, appeared like miniature mountains. The room was anything but silent. The television continued to play, the volume loud to compensate for her once limited hearing. The light from the screen flickered on the surrounding walls giving a surreal, almost artistic atmosphere. Initially, after the blow, she had twitched spasmodically, almost fit-like, but this had stopped as quickly as it had started. She had neither seen nor heard

11

anyone, she had experienced neither fear nor anguish. Even the bottle making contact with her fragile skull seemed not to register with any of her senses; there was only an immediate darkness and silence.

It would be hours before anyone might call and by then, for Betty, it would certainly be too late.

Chapter 3

Cyril's office was tidy. It always was. He required order and efficiency in his life. Removing his jacket, he placed it on a hanger before attaching it on the hook behind the door. There was a silence, a peace, that was neither claustrophobic nor was it reassuring; it brought only the usual calm that was present at times like these before the inevitable New Year storm. He paused, allowing his fingers to drum lightly on the paper-free desk before picking up the small, bronze statue, a wedding gift from his team. The figure, arm raised holding the stone tablets containing the Ten Commandments, symbolised to him strength, commitment and determination and it made him feel humble and yet proud; at this moment he now knew that he had made great progress psychologically over the festive holiday. He had finally been able to departmentalise and come to terms with demons that had plagued him for far too long.

Placing the statue back on the desk, his eyes came to rest on the dark grey filing cabinet opposite. With a degree of reluctance and yet a new found optimism, he crossed the room and slid open the top drawer. The hollow, metallic noise emphasised the fact that it was almost empty, empty apart from one item. A framed photograph stared back at him; the face of Liz Graydon still smiled as it had always done since the photograph had been buried there. The eyes laughed also, captured in that forever moment. Even from within the metal tomb, Cyril detected a radiance, a palpable energy of the woman he had known; a trusted and efficient colleague who had been taken too soon, so callously and cruelly. The guilt her murder had engendered within him too long, like the spectre at the feast. Cyril lifted the frame and held it to the light, wiping a finger across the glass. A shallow frisson of guilt churned his stomach but this time it was only like a passing breath; it was soon gone.

"Welcome back, Liz." Cyril spoke and although it was only a whisper, it was expressed out loud, a confirmation of his optimism. A smile appeared on his lips. "You've been too long in the dark, both here and in my head."

He placed the frame upright on top of the cabinet and slid the drawer closed. Movement caught his peripheral vision and he guiltily turned towards the door. Framed in the light was a diminutive figure dressed as Spiderman. Cyril paused as the guilt flushed away.

"Spiderman, do come in." Cyril crouched to the height of the superhero and a broad smile crossed his lips.

The child ran forward open armed. Cyril collected him and lifted him high.

"Does Spiderman fly or hang from fine threads of web?"

The child pointed his hand before making a sound to suggest the thread was being spun. Another shadow appeared at the door, darker and larger this time.

"Sorry, sir, he escaped, that's the trouble with

superheroes, they're difficult to watch over, slippery to catch and even more difficult to hold on to." Owen moved over and affectionately tapped his son on his bottom. "Come on, we have crime to fight." He winked at Cyril. "Popped in early, I promised to show Spiderman Daddy's desk and he wanted to surprise his Uncle Cyril. Hannah's waiting in the car. She's in work today too!" Owen glanced at the photograph on top of the cabinet and then looked at Cyril but said nothing, sensing that his boss had reached another important milestone in his psychological healing.

Cyril handed Christopher to Owen who raised him even higher. "Come on … To infinity and beyond."

"That's wrong, Daddy, that's Buzz Lightyear! Spider-Man says, 'With great power comes great responsibility.'" The last word proved more than a little difficult to pronounce but Owen helped and it was understood.

"He's growing up, Owen!"

Owen raised his eyebrows. "Too quickly, sir." He flew him through the door leaving Cyril grinning and shaking his head. His New Year had started well. Owen quickly returned. "Human remains have been found at Kex Gill, the report's there for you." He pointed to the computer. "Welcome back."

Cyril breathed out deeply as he went and sat at his desk. Within minutes Brian Smirthwaite knocked on the door.

"It's a New Year, but looks like it's going to be just like the last. We have a fatality, sir. Quite a bizarre one too. Elderly spinster, found with a severe head wound. Miss Betty Cole MBE. Eighty-three years old by all accounts." He waited to let the full title hit home. "Daughter of Squadron

Leader Sir Henry Cole." He paused again.

Cyril steepled his fingers demonstrating greater patience. "Fine title," he paused. "Is it for us at this early stage?" His frown was clearly visible.

"As I said, bizarre and that makes it very much relevant to us. The neighbour found her this morning. From the evidence it looks like an attack, robbery possibly and the person or persons were over-enthusiastic. Bottle to the head. SOCO are still present. You may not be aware, but this is the third robbery of this nature in the last two weeks, however, this one has ended up as a murder."

All this whilst you've been sitting on your arse at home, Bennett. Cyril thought, as his eyes looked across at the photograph of Liz on the filing cabinet.

"It would only be a matter of time before we saw a fatality, either through shock, heart attack or violence. This victim was a bit special, an MBE. She received the honour for charitable work but we also have this." Brian slid over a photograph taken at the scene from a file.

Cyril was disturbed just how swiftly Miss Cole had been relegated to the past as he collected the photograph. "Her legacy will remain long after she passed, Brian, let's not forget that … What the …"

"Postage stamp stuck to her forehead and if you look carefully at the wording just beneath on her skin, I'm assured it's somehow stamped or printed just over her eyebrows, it says, 'Please deliver to the Promised Land.'"

Cyril collected his glasses and inspected the photograph in greater detail, his changing facial expression demonstrated confusion. "Really?" He shook his head, looked at Brian and then back at the photograph. "Could those words be linked to her MBE, her charitable work? The Promised Land, capital letters, too. Some kind of bizarre, deliberate statement meaning her death was an organised, planned justifiable reward?" He did not wait for the answer. "Who's attending?"

"Shakti." Brian dropped the relevant details onto the desk. "What we know is in here. The usual, CCTV and house to house has been started. Interestingly, sir, the two other properties where the victims were attacked were within the boundaries of a housing estate. Just violence there; no bottle used just brute force from the evidence." He separated two further photographs showing the houses and paused. "What do you notice?"

Cyril popped on his glasses again and looked at each image. "Hand holds attached near the front door and railings on the door sides and the steps."

"Aids for the elderly. It's done for mobility, to keep folk in their homes rather than in the care system. Honourable and morally right but it blatantly advertises the nature and possible vulnerability of the occupant. Like a red light on a brothel, if you'll pardon the crude analogy, these are clear indicators to the potential thief or thieves. Easy pickings to feed a drug dependency?"

Cyril continued to look at the photographs. "What was taken?"

"The usual, cash, jewellery, even their wedding rings. The removal of jewellery from the first two victims caused injury to the fingers and ears. That's the extent, other than causing sheer fear and emotional trauma and of course ... from initial reports, nothing seems to have been removed from Cole's body. The jewellery was still there." Brian's expression was one of incredulity.

"So, nothing like this?" Cyril stabbed at the photograph of Cole's head. "No stamp or writing on either of the others."

Brian shook his head. "As I said, even her jewellery was left intact."

"Which could indicate a different perpetrator," Cyril mumbled as if he were not prepared to commit.

"The attacks also came in homes of single occupancy, and there was no alarm. Even if there had been, the attacks took place in the evenings. In one of the homes the owner had been decamped to the ground floor owing to mobility issues. They had an internal camera that could be checked by her son who lived in the Scottish borders but he saw or heard nothing from the system. Both were found when their morning carers visited the following morning."

"Can you replay the recordings? The videos should be stored in the so-called cloud or some other wizardry." Cyril's voice lacked confidence and he sounded confused, clearly uncertain of the technical facts.

"I called in a favour to get moved up the queue with our digital forensic people. They've checked but there was a glitch on that system so we can see nothing. As I said, elderly people like these are easy pickings, especially as they advertise their disability by adding handles and handrails! Maybe in the general scheme of things, these specific crimes are rare and small scale until you end up with a spate or get one like this." He tapped the photograph of Cole. "Where you end up with murder."

"I'll not wait until Shakti gets in. I want to visit now." Cyril rested his hand on the file. "Thanks, and belated Happy New Year!" He raised his eyebrows and pushed his glasses onto his head, the cynicism clear in his tone. "That's the one constant between this and the old year."

"What's that, sir?"

"We'll never be out of work."

Chapter 4

The blue and white tape fluttered across the driveway of the house situated along Duchy Road. A CSI van was still there, positioned on the roadside. Frost had started to cover the windscreen, it had been there some time. An officer standing before the line of tape looked frozen as he shifted his weight from one foot to the other. Cyril climbed from the warmth of his car and immediately understood why; the wind chill was harsh. He nodded as he showed his ID.

"Not the best of days for your job." Cyril's words seemed to state the obvious but they brought a degree of recognition.

"Could be worse, sir, it could be snowing." The officer blew onto his gloves. "I've dressed in more layers than a mille-feuille, just don't ask me to run anywhere!" He grinned with little sincerity.

Cyril tapped his shoulder. "Good man. Is the Crime Scene Manager inside?"

The officer signed him in as he nodded. "Another officer too." He checked the log. "DC Misra. Are you the SIO?"

Cyril shook his head, tapped his gloved hands together and started to walk down the gravel driveway. He noticed the multiple narrow track marks leading from the house and he assumed they had been made by the gurney used to collect and remove the body. The large, detached stone house was imposing and the garden well-tended considering the time of year. The house had been built in the height of Harrogate's prosperity when quality, fine detail and craftsmanship were at their peak. Cyril looked for handrails and other possible tell-tale signs that might have informed the perpetrator of the owner's age and vulnerability but saw none. He also noted an alarm box placed high on the gable end; it contradicted what Brian had told him. A double garage was built away from the house, it too was stone and substantial. Even though it was cold, the front door was propped open. He waited at the threshold and called. Shakti appeared.

"The deceased was removed an hour ago. Have you seen the photograph?"

"Indeed. I take it she's at the morgue and not the Promised …" He stopped himself.

They both walked on step plates until arriving at the living room. A criss-cross of tape was stretched at angles across the door. Cyril paused as his eyes mapped the room. The curtains were still drawn and the television was on but now the room lights were enhanced by the investigators' free-standing LED lamps. The blood-stained rug seemed unusually dark. Although the apparent brown stain showed little resemblance to blood, Cyril felt his stomach churn and a sudden flush of warmth flooded to his face. Body fluids of any kind in any setting had always affected him, particularly if they were his own.

"Do we have entry and exit points?" Cyril looked down

the corridor and then towards the open front door, happy to keep his eyes away from the carpet.

"It appears it was the back door. It was not forced so we can only presume it was left unlocked."

Cyril did not like assumption nor did he believe in guess work. "Did she have an external key safe and if so, is it still intact?"

Shakti's face revealed the answer. "If there is, we haven't found it yet but the initial part of the investigation was carried out in the dark so it was unlikely to be found." She predicted the next question. "She doesn't have a carer so there may not have been the need for one. She was, according to a neighbour, still very much alert, still drives and shops. The only disability is her hearing, hence the loud television."

"Once CSI are happy, I suggest a good search before they go. Key safes can be in the strangest of places. The neighbour?" Cyril let his eyes focus on a large painting on the wall at the base of the stairs – another line of tape was attached to the newel post and an ornately carved mahogany chair had been positioned to prevent anyone going up. The gilt frame was large and in keeping with the style of the painting and the house. Removing his glasses from his pocket, he slid them on his nose before inspecting the picture.

"Lives next door. He's about the same age. He walks his dog and noticed the curtains were drawn." Shakti stood behind Cyril, looked at the landscape and yawned.

"What time was that?" Cyril leaned closer to the canvas.

"About six thirty. Although it was dark and still early, he realised there was a problem as her curtains were closed downstairs. Something she never did, always drew them back when she went to bed. She had apparently remarked to Mr Crookson that if ever they were closed in the morning to call in and check, which he did. He knocked at the front door but there was no response so he went round the back. Finding the door ajar he went in. He rang 999 from the phone here." She pointed to the phone on the hall stand.

"Reginald Brundrit. Liverpool born artist. Fascinating man, Shakti. He eventually saw the light like many and settled in Yorkshire. Beautiful. It's like looking through a window in time."

"Mr Crookson found her." Shakti stressed again. "Mr Rodney Crookson, her neighbour."

"Yes, and phoned from the landline here." He pointed in the general direction without taking his eyes from the painting. "How is he?"

"He seemed fine, just mentioned she'd had a good innings as if he were discussing the weather! I was rather non-plussed if I were to be honest."

"DCI Bennett?" Shakti and Cyril turned towards the lounge door. The CSI stood just in the hallway. She was holding part of a bottle, the murder weapon. A small brush handle pushed through the bottle's neck cradling the upper part. She held it horizontally so he could see the label. "Sherry. A good one too. We found a ring stain where it had sat in the kitchen on the work surface, so it's possible the killer collected it on entering. We believe he may have drunk some of the contents. There were traces of sherry on her and spread around her immediate surroundings. We know from experience that striking a victim with a partially full bottle has a far more devastating impact than that of an empty one." She turned and looked into the room before turning back. "The stopper is still on the carpet. We'll check for prints and DNA as soon as."

Cyril frowned, maybe he had been upsetting himself over a sherry stain and not blood after all.

The CSI continued. "The driveway is predominantly gravel but there's a small paved area near the back door and paving leading to the garage. A number of people have entered the house through the back door. We could see no definitive prints, but we will continue to check, the same with the carpet in the hall and the lounge. Once we've completed the initial sweep, we'll fine comb the room. We'll also check the other rooms. Nothing, as far as we can see at this stage, seems to be missing, everything appears orderly. However, until we know what was in the house, we're purely guessing. None of the drawers or cupboards has been opened, from what we can see. Normally during cases like this if the place had been searched the perpetrator would leave them open and not waste time closing them."

Cyril moved closer and looked at the bottle. Removing his phone, he took a photograph of the label. "Can you confirm the base of the bottle has an indent, I thought it was called a pontil but I was recently corrected, it's known as a punt."

"It does but not a large one." She seemed confused at his question.

"The deeper the punt, the heavier the glass bottle."

"Right, if you say so," she continued. "The doctor believes death occurred before midnight. The television has been on since then, however, the volume has been reduced."

"Thanks, I'll leave DC Misra with you." Cyril left via the still open front door, ensuring he walked on the step plates. The cold was immediate but within minutes he was at Crookson's house. The door opened partially, obstructed by a security chain.

"DCI Bennett. Mr Crookson, I believe?" Cyril thrust his ID into the gap. "It's about your neighbour. You found her."

The door closed partially and then opened. "First time I've used that chain in quite some time. This is usually a safe area. These days, however, things are changing too bloody rapidly what with kids with knives, drugs and illegals. Christ, and to think we would have once been proud to fight for this great nation. Gone to hell in a handcart and you men don't seem to be able to do bugger all about it. Good thrashing many of them need if you ask me. Never did us any harm and whilst they're at it they could bring back conscription. Then the little toerags would be able to discern right from wrong, put polish on their shoes or they'd get a kick up the bloody arse."

Cyril waited patiently, allowing much of what was said to wash over him. "May I come in or have you more comments about today's society?"

"Sorry, how rude of me. I can't complain if I allow my standards and manners to slip. Do accept my apologies. Bennett, you said?"

"Detective Chief Inspector Bennett."

Bennett looked at the elderly man. His tweed jacket, checked shirt, green tie and neatly pressed cavalry twill trousers gave him a military air. There was a shine to his shoes so at least he practised some of the things he preached. The living room of the large Victorian detached home was as Cyril had expected, ordered with a lifetime's possessions that seemed to reflect an interesting past. Mainly antique yet particularly stylish, expensive and in keeping.

"May I offer you tea?" A female voice came from down the corridor. An elegantly dressed woman was standing at the far end. "I'm making it for us, it's been a rather frenetic morning as you can well imagine, so it would be no bother. Coffee if you prefer."

"That's the memsahib, don't let her catch me saying that!" Crookson flicked out his tongue and shrugged his shoulders as if admonishing himself. "Jennifer, the better half."

"Thank you, yes. Tea would be perfect."

"We might get a scone if we're lucky. Do sit. How may I help."

The conversation flowed and Cyril gleaned little more than what Shakti had reported earlier.

"That's what she always said, Detective Chief Inspector, if my curtains are still drawn in the morning pop in and check I haven't kicked the bucket. Bloody shocked to see that she had. Careful what you wish for, what? Couldn't believe what I was seeing, with what looked like a stamp on her forehead and there was something written but I didn't have my glasses, struggled dialling you people too."

Jennifer started to become tearful as she served the tea and hearing the matter-of-fact way in which the discovery of the body was described, she quickly returned to the kitchen. She, for one, was clearly shaken by the death of her neighbour which brought Crookson's seeming lack of concern into stark contrast. There was an unusual calm, best described as normality, possibly as if the murder of a close neighbour was an everyday occurrence.

"If I can help in any way, Detective Chief Inspector, do ask. You would be most welcome."

"I'd be grateful if you would say nothing about what you saw in there today. The Press may call, usually they'll phone and try to catch you off guard. What you witnessed is critical evidence we need to keep from the public."

"Mum's the word, Detective Chief Inspector, mum's the word. Careless talk and all that. I have to say Jennifer makes a perfect scone." He dabbed the crumbs left on his plate with his licked finger.

Cyril just looked at the man. He was lost for words.

***

"Nothing has been caught on CCTV. A petty crime that necessitated the murder of an elderly spinster in her own home is most barbaric." April Richmond tapped the whiteboard, focusing the attention of the two officers in the room as she lifted and scrutinised briefly the details of the other two attacks reported. They were both similar. "Knock and wait for the door to open and then overpower the victim. Frighten them silly, take what can be used or sold and leave them incapable of calling for help. A simple mask would guarantee there would be no chance of identification. Whether we should, or even can, dedicate valuable resources to investigate associative evidence is always debatable. It should be remembered the houses were frequented by a number of carers, sometimes four times a day, bringing a high percentage of human footfall to each home. Collecting biological and physical evidence would be difficult and time-consuming. However, with a death comes a different set of priorities."

"So, prevention is not better than cure? It would seem to many that it would only be a matter of time before we had a ..." DC Stuart Park mumbled loud enough for the group to hear but did not finish his contribution as he inspected a rogue fingernail on his left hand.

"Resources are never finite, Stuart, as well you know. Warnings have been issued and carers have imparted those instructions to their clients but we all know that some advice will have fallen on stony ground. The media has also reported the death both locally and nationally and that might send the killer to ground."

Stuart pointed to a photograph on the board. "It's the clues that were left, the stamp and the writing that causes me grave concern. From my experience, and granted that's limited, it's as if whoever did this is taunting us or is justifying the act of brutality to themselves or maybe even the victim. I asked myself why that might be and the only answer I could think of was the wording justified the act, it made it right! I can't help thinking that whoever did this believed they were helping them along the way to a better place, bizarre as that might sound." He paused momentarily. "Or it was purely revenge ... fulfilment of a promise, a promise made in the past."

There was an appreciative pause as if those in the room were trying to comprehend Stuart's thinking. There was a degree of logic to both ideas. Nothing was added to the boards other than the facts.

April broke the uncomfortable silence. "The post-mortem confirms the wording to the forehead was stamped and they assume it may be one of those old-style ink pad and rubber stamps. Red indelible ink. I've checked and that type of product is still produced. Enquiries with those manufacturers are ongoing but like many things these days, these products are made in China. The wording is unusual and hopefully would be memorable to whoever sold it. Forensic evidence shows the body had been moved after being struck … rolled over from landing on their front to being placed on their back. All to do with blood spatter and the position of her feet apparently. They believe the victim was repositioned to facilitate the stamping on the forehead. Death came from one strike with the bottle."

"Was she dead when the writing or the printing took place?" Park sat up as he asked the question.

"There's no confirmation either way as far as the report states. Why do you ask?" April questioned with a degree of caution after his last statement.

"If you hadn't successfully killed her, then the words chosen would be irrelevant, surely. 'Please deliver to the Promised Land' seems to suggest that by the moment of writing it, she had been despatched, or considering the postage stamp …" he held up a photograph showing the stamp attached to her forehead, "… should I say posted? Duty paid!" His comments resonated within the room. There seemed a callousness in the words, not in the way Park conveyed his thoughts but in the realisation of the possibility of truth. Considering the evidence before them, the point was brought home. "Was the killer aware of the work she'd done or still did? Is it some obscene sign of gratitude? Deliverance?"

April mumbled the name 'Joshua' but regained her composure and responded quickly. "There was nothing removed, her jewellery was still intact ... so why?" Her facial expression clearly showed disgust at a motiveless death and disbelief it should happen to a generous, kind, elderly woman! "And to mark the woman with a stamp—"

"Maybe to conceal what it was ... make it look like a robbery, a robbery like the others," Stuart added. "The others have been in the local press and we do get copycat crimes."

"Star gazing, philosophising or even guessing the motive at this stage I don't think is of any value. What is, in my mind, is the evidence we have and to be honest we don't have much at this stage." Shakti deliberately looked at Park and then back to April as if seeking an ally. She was successful in her quest.

"We work the evidence and as more comes in, we act." Turning she wrote the name 'Joshua' on the whiteboard. She was going to add more but stopped herself. What she wanted to write might be seen to be too obscure.

Chapter 5

Philip Spencer locked the door of the charity shop before weighing the bunch of keys in his hand and slipping them into his coat pocket. The dark winter evenings came early and the customers were few. The closing of the metal roller shutters on a shop further up Cambridge Street echoed loudly; a sound like a drum roll signalled another shop had closed for the day. Across the pedestrian street, work continued under a plethora of spotlights to convert what was once a large section of shops into new apartments. Philip, a man who had witnessed many changes in his life, saw little to commend the vision of the town's planners; even the street lights, the old-style lanterns that befitted the spa town were being replaced in certain areas with modern, more efficient LED lights, either to save money or to save the planet. Charity shops, barbers, fast food and vape shops seemed to be on the increase as the independent and more exclusive shops for which Harrogate had become famous, were gradually becoming a thing of the past. He shook his head, resigned to the fact he could change none of these things. He tapped his pocket receiving reassurance the keys were there before moving off. Home was a twenty-minute walk away.

Years ago, the walk from the centre of Harrogate to Dragon Parade, a home he had enjoyed for over forty years, would have taken him ten minutes but at seventy-five, his chosen pace was more leisurely. He would call into Asda, select something for an evening meal and then head home.

**

DCI Cyril Bennett walked home from the police station taking his usual route. He paused at the point at which two footpaths crossed the Stray. The intense dark of the early evening enveloped the vast area broken only by the occasional lantern's glow. The noise of the traffic was a constant, an urban tinnitus occasionally broken by a siren or car horn, an interruption that brought him back to the present as he continued his walk. Soon the ginnel appeared, the dim passage that linked West Park to Robert Street, a dark space that was always a micro climate whatever the season, a small wind tunnel and in some ways a magic gateway leading to the sanctuary of home.

**

Philip Spencer turned his collar to the cold and thrust his hands deep into his pockets as he walked towards Station Parade. In one dark, closed shop doorway he spotted a huddled figure protected by grubby bags and cocooned within a dirty sleeping bag. These apparitions, the homeless, were becoming regular roosters in many areas of Harrogate's centre. The man's eyes were almost hidden beneath the peak of a cap and they stared out neither focusing on him nor the others making their way home. Philip paused. He thought he recognised the almost hidden face but then doubted himself. He spent his days volunteering in a charity shop and yet here, not one hundred yards away, was evidence that maybe charity needed to be closer to home. Searching his inner jacket pocket, he found what he was looking for and held out a fiver before letting it fall into a paper cup sitting in one of the many fabric furls of the sleeping bag. A hand moved in thanks but no words were spoken. *I can have beans on toast tonight,* Philip thought as he moved away. It also meant he avoided popping into the supermarket but more importantly, someone else would eat. He felt a warm sense of satisfaction as he crossed the road, negotiating the slow-moving traffic with a degree of nimbleness that defied his age. Once safely across his progress slowed.

A fine, mist-like, freezing drizzle began to sweep across Dragon Parade as Philip slipped his key into the lock. The hallway felt warm as he flicked on the light. Closing the door, he leaned against it as if helping to form a barricade from the outside world and he let his eyes close. Although it was his house, it was no longer his home, not since his wife had passed. From that point it had grown hollow and cold, it was now simply a house filled with memories, a place where there was no real future, only a past.

The noise, a cough, faint but still discernible came from upstairs. The memories flooded back as he thought of his wife, Patricia, struggling with the debilitating, late stages of mesothelioma. His heart beat faster. He listened again, his head tilted towards the staircase. The silence was deafening and his pulse seemed to flush through his body and bounce within his ears, dominating his senses.

"Patricia?" The word was spoken with a nervous, curious uncertainty. There was no reply and after a few moments the silence only brought a smile to his lips, in some ways it was a relief. "You're a sad and silly old bugger, Philip Spencer. You need a scotch to clear that troubled head of yours and warm the cockles." He giggled childlike to himself.

Removing his coat, flat cap and scarf he carefully hung them on the pegs by the door and moved into the kitchen. Collecting a tumbler, he poured a generous measure before adding some dry ginger from the fridge. Leaving the almost full bottle on the table, he knew this drink would not be his last as he moved into the room he had always called the parlour. The chair, his chair, was inviting. He flicked on the gas fire and it burst into life. "Cheers Pat—"

"Patricia isn't here." A faint voice interrupted his toast, an audible gesture that would be the last words he would ever hear. A gasp and squeal, guttural and instinctive burst from Philip's lips as the tumbler slipped from his hand before striking the fire hearth and shattering. As if in slow motion, Philip's limp body followed before crumpling into a heap, creating a shape that was not too dissimilar from that of the doorway sleeper.

Chapter 6

David Owen moved quickly towards Cyril's office, eager to convey the latest report.

"We have another one." He glanced at the piece of paper on which he had scribbled his notes. "Philip Spencer. Lives on Dragon Parade. Seventy-five years old. Sent to the Promised Land like the previous victim." Owen raised his eyebrows.

The word *victim* seemed to focus Cyril's mind as he stood and held out his hand for the sheet Owen was holding; the ring stains from a coffee mug did not detract.

"He did voluntary work in the charity shop on Cambridge Street, has done for a year or more. He closed up the place last night and we're checking CCTV to see the route he took home. Officers are going door to door for eye-witness or doorbell camera evidence on Dragon Parade too. If he left when he normally does, it would be about a quarter to six."

"When was he found and by whom?" Cyril propped himself against his desk.

"Milkman, can you believe. They're a rare breed these days. A Darren Styles. He's been delivering to the

Spencers for years and he saw the front door open which had never happened before. He knocked and as no one answered he popped in only to discover the body. Strangely, it was the day Spencer normally paid his bill. Darren, the milkman, usually called in the evening when people were at home." Owen pointed to his notes.

Cyril read further. "5.55 am. Very specific."

"When interviewed he mentioned that he listens to Radio Four every day and Tweet of the Day had just started, that's—" He did not finish once he noted Cyril's expression.

"Five to six, Owen, Tweet of the Day, a fascinating insight into the sounds of birds if you've not heard it." Cyril's response seemed rather smug. "No. Right! Anyway, that allowed him to pinpoint the time accurately. Go on."

"The same red ink wording is stamped on his forehead and there's also a postage stamp as in the previous case. Strangely, it's one without the new barcoding. First class. CSI are there now and the first responder paramedic certified him dead. The milkman is coming in once he's finished his round. He seemed a little troubled by the experience but insisted he continue. 'The milk must get through', his words."

"Funny that, Owen, the two finders of the bodies were both seemingly unaffected by their discoveries even though the circumstances are bizarre. I wonder why that is?"

Owen just shrugged his shoulders. "Amazing how many dog walkers and joggers find them. A milkman? I've never known that before."

"Use Room Two as an Incident Room and get in the necessary staff. I don't want the details of the postage stamps or the wording leaking." He instinctively pointed to his forehead, "especially to the press."

Owen immediately thought of Peter Kay, phone, laptop, phone and the comedian turning his hand into a phone or pretending to tap away at imaginary keys.

"Are you listening, Owen?"

"Yes, postage stamps. You don't want it leaking, sir."

"Get in touch with Styles and ensure he mentions it to no one, providing he hasn't already spread it to half the people on his milk round."

Owen collected his notes.

"I see we have more information on the remains found at Kex Gill. According to the magic of scientific technology, it looks like they were interred in the late sixties or early seventies. Male and female but as yet we are unsure if they were buried at the same time as the find area was quite spread out." Owen tapped the keyboard and brought up the latest file. "There's evidence of trauma to one of the found scapula, possibly the result of a spade or an axe strike. Whether this was pre or post death is unclear at this stage. Further tests are being carried out for DNA. The search for those missing at or around that date has brought up eight people. As yet we do not have an accurate age of either person found. Dental records are also being checked. Once DNA is assured, we can check against relatives of those who've gone missing. We're working locally and then spreading our search wider as the site is so close to what was a major transport route."

Cyril returned to his chair.

"I checked and because the area was close to the A59 I thought they might be either students or prostitutes ... well one of them." Owen waited for a response but none came. "There's a lane at the back of the discovery area and ideal for some sexual recreation but it was something Hannah said. In the sixties and seventies hitch-hiking was considered acceptable and to a certain extent safe. I'm sure for the lone female that might not be the case, but blokes or a couple? Did you ever try it, sticking out the thumb?" He demonstrated. "Hitch hiking when you were young?"

"What are you suggesting, Owen? I was not even a twinkle at the time, so no is the answer but it might surprise you to know I have friends who did." He frowned at Owen receiving a chuckle in return. "Don't forget, my young subordinate, danger comes in many forms so we often believe the hitch-hikers were the probable victims but there were cases where the driver fell victim too. You're right, of course, anyone hitching a ride suddenly becomes anonymous until they reach their chosen destination. They're at the mercy of the driver and the route they take. Their requested destination might not be where they end up! Should anything happen the body ... and their possessions could be separated by many miles, making identification difficult. Also, at that time, let's not forget, there were no such things as mobile phones, CCTV or DNA. It was easy to vanish or make others disappear. If we have photographs of the missing persons from this period, sixties to late seventies, I want them on an incident board with as much information as possible. Sooner or later, we'll be in a position to narrow those down, locate families and check DNA samples until we have a match." He raised his glasses and secured them on his head. "You'll lead that and I'll put April on these two and make sure she speaks to our milkman." Cyril paused.

"Styles, Darren Styles," Owen added.

"Right. Never rains but it pours, Owen. Welcome to the New Year."

"Owen turned to leave but then frowned and turned back. "Who's Job and who are the comforters?"

"Why do you ask?"

"Something Dr Green said at the crime scene."

"Job was a man who lost everything and was comforted by men who came to help but who really brought no comfort at all. So, the term Job's comforter is used for those people who want to bring support but do not."

"Dr Green apologised for being one because he felt as though he brought no real answers. I was going to ask April when I saw her. Thanks."

Here endeth the first lesson, came to mind. "While I think on, Owen, I also want Harry Nixon to search out aerial photographs of the area around Kex Gill for the period they believe the bodies went into the ground. Let's see what the terrain was like then. You'll also need to be at Spencer's autopsy." Cyril checked his watch, shook his wrist and looked again. "You know the time?"

Owen nodded. "April, sir, she's attending." He left without looking back whilst Cyril grabbed his coat.

***

Cambridge Street was busy. At the junction with Market Place, a street musician was singing opera and a small group of people had congregated despite the cold. Cyril paused briefly to listen. The song echoed within the constraints of the buildings, her voice, strong and powerful; he would have liked to have heard more but walked on. As he opened the door of the charity shop, he noticed there were three people shopping and two female assistants. He approached the closer of the two and showed his ID.

"DCI Bennett. I'm sorry about your colleague."

The assistant lowered her head and nodded. "I was so shocked. I only heard an hour ago. It sent me all wobbly, I can tell you. He was a lovely man, worked here for a long time. He'd do anything for anyone." She forced a smile. "Why would someone want to hurt such a lovely man?"

Cyril could not answer her question. "Did he always lock up on the days he worked?"

"Yes, always insisted the other colleague go and he sorted out, closed up particularly when the dark nights come. That's the kind of gentleman he was, always put others before himself and there are few who do these days, Mr Bennett. Sonya was with him yesterday. He insisted she go at just before five."

"Sonya?"

"Another volunteer. She's too upset to come in but I rang her this morning. She should be in tomorrow, today should be one of her volunteer days, but she couldn't face it. I'm happy to cover for her. She'd do the same for me, you know." She smiled again, this time with a degree more sincerity.

"Did Mr Spencer have any issues with customers recently? I know it's a charity shop but I'm sure you're not immune to the odd problem customer or shop lifter."

The shaking of her head answered his question. "If we did, he would always handle the problem. No, I never saw him have any real issues." There was a pause and Cyril gave her time to think. "He did change, in himself, when his wife passed away but that's normal, I suppose. He became different, sad might be the best way to describe him. He was quieter, as if the wind had been taken from his sails. He smiled less whereas before he liked to tell a joke or two."

"Did he have any hobbies? We're trying to track any relatives but as far as we know he had no siblings, nor did they have any children."

There was a pause. The assistant tightened her mouth and looked across at the other assistant who was now busy with a customer. "I don't know if I'm speaking out of turn but he once told me that his wife, Patricia, he always called her that, never shortened it to Pat, that she'd had a child out of wedlock before they were wed, not his. He'd had a sherry or two the other Christmas and told me that as a secret. He was such a sensitive, and in many ways, generous … no, I think the better term would be charitable. Not many men would have remained in a relationship on discovering that."

"Did he say more about the child?" Cyril moved closer to the counter.

"A boy, goodness he'll be a man now I assume, but I don't know any more about his personal circumstances. He obviously loved his wife very much and he always spoke of her fondly. It really was a blow when she died."

"Does the shop have CCTV?" Cyril scanned the room as he spoke.

"It has cameras but they're from the previous occupants. They don't work and I believe they were left there as a deterrent. It's a charity shop after all."

Cyril left her his contact details, thanked her for her co-operation at such a difficult time and left the shop. He would take the shortest route to Dragon Parade assuming that would be the way Spencer would walk. The opera singer had gone. He glanced at a doorway littered with what appeared to be full yet dirty shopping bags and an empty sleeping bag. The words of the assistant came immediately to mind, 'generous and charitable'. Betty Cole had received her MBE for charitable work and here, the second victim was also seen as charitable above all else, both in his actions and within his personal life and circumstances. This had to be relevant to the investigation.

The officer attending Spencer's address opened the front door for Cyril. The hallway to the home could be classed as tired but not dirty. There was no dust on the mahogany table in the hallway. Although CSI had finished their investigation, he still slipped on a pair of nitrile gloves and followed the crime scene procedure. He had read briefly the report and knew the layout of the ground floor rooms. He scanned the room where the attack had taken place, the blood stain on the carpet remained. There were too many similarities with the first case to dismiss the idea it was committed by one and the same. He collected a framed collection of photographs from the sideboard. The collage of images showed different times in the life of a couple. It made him think of Liz Graydon, she too had gone but her laughing face lived on, trapped in the moment when life was real and good. It was as Spencer's colleague had said, they seemed ideally matched and happy but then, we seldom keep photographs of unhappy times, not in frames and certainly not displayed on sideboards.

As Cyril closed the front door his attention was drawn to a man talking to the officer at the gate. They both turned as Cyril approached.

"This is DCI Bennett. He may be better able to help you." The officer stood away as he spoke.

Cyril held out his hand. "How may I help?"

"I live there." The man pointed to the house next door within the terraced row. "I'm his immediate neighbour, and have been for some time. I like to think I was a good friend. I've spoken to the police this morning after he was found. If you've a minute or two I'd appreciate a word. It would be better to talk in the warm in mine."

Cyril followed.

***

Darren Styles sat opposite April in the Interview Room. He was still dressed in his Kay's Dairy jacket, his hands cupped a paper cup of coffee.

"This sounds daft but I wasn't really shocked. I thought at first that he'd done it himself, suicide like. He'd never been his old self since Pat died. He was still amicable but not the same man. Used to laugh and have a joke before but then … Bloody sad." He shook his head demonstrating his disbelief.

"Did you see anyone?" April asked.

"Loads of folk, it wasn't really early for those going to work. It was just dark and bloody freezing and seeing that his door was wide open and there was a light from the living room it seemed wrong. I've just said how cold it was at that time so it struck me as daft and odd and so out of character if you know what I mean. I didn't just go in, I knocked and shouted. When I heard nothing I investigated and found him on the carpet. There was quite a bit of blood. I rang 999 straight away and waited for the first people to come."

"Do you know if Mr Spencer had anyone stay recently? Do you know of any relatives?"

Darren pulled a face as if he were giving the questions a lot of thought. "A few weeks back he wanted extra milk and he also wanted me to leave eggs and a loaf, that was very unusual. Strangely, when I called to collect my money that week, I sensed that someone else was in the house too."

"Sensed or saw?"

"As I said, sensed," he said defensively but then relaxed. "Normally he loves a chat at the door, can talk for ages. More often than not I have to drag myself away or I'd never get my collection done or get home, but on this occasion, he just handed me the money, thanked me and closed the door. Funny that. Totally out of the ordinary; rude really and he was never rude. It was as if he didn't want me to see inside or see anyone. Totally out of character, like."

"Could they, whoever you sensed was there, have been a relative? Does he even have relatives?"

Darren shrugged his shoulders. "Maybe that was one. I don't know. I just deliver his milk and as I say, I only sensed he had a visitor."

April thanked him. Darren finished his coffee and left.

***

Cyril had slipped off his coat as invited.

"It really shakes you up when a murder is committed on

44

your doorstep, especially when it's an old man and a good man who's been killed."

Cyril rested his hands on his knees and looked at Spencer's neighbours. "Did you have something you wanted to tell me in confidence, Mr Hussain, other than giving Mr Spencer a glowing character reference?"

Hussain looked at his wife and then back at Cyril. "No, no. Sorry, I was just setting some, what do you say, perspective, yes. You see it's a bit delicate. I've, well we've known the couple for quite some years. They were kind to us when we moved in which is more than can be said for some of the residents, you'll understand. In this type of house, you hear things through the walls, sometimes just the plug being pulled from the socket, or laughter, or music but I'm talking about shouting, high-pitched shouting."

"A couple having a row? It's normal." Cyril believed he was wasting valuable time.

Hussain looked again at his wife and she spoke. "You see we never heard a peep when Patricia was alive, not in that sense, shouting. It only happened after she passed away. As if he's angry, shouting at himself or life itself. I know only too well, as I was a district nurse and I understand that death can play dreadful tricks on those who are left but this—" She removed her handkerchief and brought it to her eye. "In a strange way, it didn't sound like him."

"Whoever it was, you're not sure if it were Philip Spencer's voice? Could there have been someone with him?"

Both shook their heads in unison. Mrs Hussain paused before responding. "We don't know. It's been a worry since it started and neither of us felt comfortable in asking him if things were alright. We could only go by appearances and whenever we saw him, he seemed fine. Patricia once told me that she'd had a child, a boy, before she met Philip. It caused a great deal of trouble with her parents as well as destroying her hopes and ambitions. I believe the birth was so traumatic that's why she never had other children. She cried so much when she told me. I just wondered if Fraser, that was what she called the child, I remember it clearly, Fraser Melling, Melling was her maiden name. He could have been the one in the house."

"When did this start?" Cyril took out a notepad and pencil.

Mrs Hussain explained, whilst looking at her husband for reassurance. "Some time after Patricia passed. It wasn't every day nor every week, best to say occasionally at first but it was becoming more frequent."

"Did you see anyone come or go?"

"No. That's why my husband believed he might be shouting out in frustration, anger or sadness."

Mr Hussain swiftly added. "As I've said, when I met him out, he was his usual self, even though he may not have been the same as before his wife died. To be kind, let's just say a bit of him had died too."

"And you saw nobody enter or leave?"

"We're not busybodies, Detective Chief Inspector, but we do always try to be good neighbours and watch out for others." Hussain again glanced at his wife.

"So, you never mentioned it?"

"Goodness gracious, no," Mr Hussain remonstrated. "That would have been rude and intrusive. On hearing the sad news, we felt a degree of remorse and maybe we should have said something to someone. We're sorry if withholding this has been in any way partly responsible for the tragic circumstances."

"Not at all. What could you do? Did he know she confided in you about the child?"

"I don't know. He certainly said nothing to me." Mr Hussain glanced at his wife and then back at Cyril.

"Let me ask one final question for now. Was the noise always at the same time of day and from the same part of the house?"

"It usually occurred evenings, and sometimes late evenings. Never during the day." Hussain looked for confirmation and his wife nodded. "Occasionally we heard it from the bedroom that's next to ours but mainly it was from downstairs. His parlour, he used to call it."

Cyril sat for a moment allowing the information to digest.

"I only hope we haven't spoken out of turn." Hussain slipped an arm around his wife's shoulders.

Cyril stood, put on his coat before jotting down their telephone details. He thanked them whilst reassuring them they had done the right thing and then left. On closing the door, the chill of the late morning air struck him as much as the information he had just received. The trembling in his gut had signalled an alarm he knew he could not ignore.

Chapter 7

Harry Nixon added four aerial photographs onto the whiteboards, attaching them with different coloured magnets. The images were taken at varying periods. The latest, a few months before the road works commenced, the first, in the late 1960s. Surprisingly, the images were all colour and shown from a similar angle. Printed screenshots of Google maps and street view of the location had also been added.

"Hall Lane has always been there and has remained relatively unchanged since the period our search begins. However, the A59 has had quite a number of changes, not to the actual route, not the tarmac but what lies to either side. You can see there's quite a considerable area of woodland to the right side. This extends beyond the stream. It also varies in density. You can also see from the aerial photograph taken in 1968 there was a hard stand, a rough, gravel layby just before another stream crosses below the road in a culvert. There's neither a fence nor a wall so for anyone stopping there the woodland was easily accessible. In later photographs, that layby disappears but there is now one higher up."

Owen scrutinised the images. "The trees don't seem to have changed, as if their growth has been stunted."

"I spoke with a tree chap, an arborist, who knew the area. It's to do with the ground, the fact there are so many trees and that they've been allowed to grow so closely together. It's on land not belonging to the highways and they make a perfect visual and soundproof barrier for the house that's just up above and set away from the road. You wouldn't have known it was there until the trees came down for the new Kex Gill bypass."

"So, do we have evidence to suggest that the bodies could have been disposed of at this location?" Owen looked closely at the photograph as his finger struck the spot.

"There was opportunity to park, the road then being much less used than today; night time it was probably very quiet. I have statistics to show the A59 had much less of a traffic flow considering it was a major route. Fewer cars, a lot fewer humans then too. If the driver took the victims there, went into the wooded area for nocturnal recreation, then they were already concealed."

Owen interrupted. "The bones of a sheep were also found close to the remains. They are round about the same period so there's a possibility it was dumped over the burial site as a distraction if anyone happened to nip in for a piss or … Sorry, go on."

"The layby being in the same place meant the site of the bodies would be close together as they were discovered. There may also be more to find. At the time, if the first body wasn't discovered then it could have been considered safe to dispose of more. There's been a suggestion to bring in a cadaver dog to do a sweep and then metal detect the area.

Kind of belt and braces before the site is given back to the road builders."

"Dr Green suggested they would detect for metal objects when I first met with him," Owen suggested.

"Only around the area where the bones were discovered, not the whole area. We need a whole area sweep." Harry looked towards Owen. "As SIO it's your call, of course."

Owen nodded his agreement as he glanced across at the photographs of the people who had gone missing around the time it was believed the deaths had occurred, whilst at the same time considering the costs involved. "When I chatted to Dr Green, the forensic anthropologist, he highlighted the extent of rotted and decomposing roots and branches. As far as I'm aware, rotting vegetation could make finding very old bones difficult for the dog to detect, too many distractions. I'll pass it by Flash."

DCI Cyril Bennett had received the nickname 'Flash' from his earliest days in the force. Bennett had always been known as Flash in the Force as he progressed through the ranks. Many presumed, quite incorrectly, that it was because of his penchant for good tailoring and neatness. In the early days of his career, Cyril Bennett had carried the sobriquet 'Gordon' after an American playboy, Gordon Bennett, who enjoyed nothing more than racing cars and aircraft and collecting beautiful women. The Gordon Bennett Tourist Trophy was awarded on the Isle of Man for one of their suicide races at the beginning of the twentieth century but it was for cars and not motorcycles. From Gordon came Flash Gordon which became just Flash. This information was now lost to many in the mists of time and yet few would dare use the sobriquet to his face.

"Harry, if we were to use a dog and even if it's not successful, I agree and suggest we get some metal detectorists in. It's been done before in other police authorities, using a detectorist group to help alongside. The good Dr Green suggested if the bodies were just dumped in a hole, there might be metal objects in or amongst their possessions and finding these might lead to other evidence or discovering the identity of those found. Whatever we do, we need to do it quickly as there's pressure to get the construction work restarted. Whatever's decided, the land area will need thoroughly investigating from where the trees commenced and ended." He stabbed a finger on the photograph. "From here to say … here. The breadth of the search is determined by the road on one side and the extent of what was woodland to the other. Can I leave that with you, Harry?" Owen did not wait for the reply.

"Detectorists? Where does one find them on a cold and frosty Tuesday?" Nixon mused but his words fell on deaf ears. "Ours is not to reason why …"

***

April checked the clock on the wall and then the screen. The pathologist, Dr Julie Pritchett, Cyril's wife, looked up from behind the Perspex visor and smiled. "Good to have your company, April. You drew the short straw I take it? Thought it would be Owen. Can you hear me, okay?"

"I'm SIO on this case." April gave the thumbs up. There seemed a lot of activity around the prostrate body and the process appeared to be a well-rehearsed ballet, a performance she had remembered from the countless other procedures she had witnessed. Everything removed from the body was carefully photographed and weighed.

"That's quite some blow to the head and I suspect there was more than one, April. It has all the markings of a solid domed object. I believe Forensics have discovered skin fragments on the bottle found at the scene. Whether the blows were enough to cause death we shall have to wait and see what the body reveals. However, there's damage to the right lateral area, the temporal, sphenoid bones as well as the zygomatic arch. There's clear depression and step deformity of the bone. The head may well have been moving to look behind when struck. I would say it was with some force. There's periorbital ecchymosis as well as facial asymmetry making me believe the head was struck more than the once. Looking at the photographs taken at the scene, the damage to the left-hand side, also severe, was caused as the body fell onto the edge of the ceramic fire surround. I shall expect we'll find evidence of intracranial hematoma, maybe traumatic hematoma. The evidence of bleeding you can see here." She pointed to the side of the head. "It's from the damage caused to the inner ear."

April nodded, trying to take in what she was seeing and hearing; she had enough experience and knowledge to follow the diagnosis. "Strange how the victim's face was not damaged, the forehead particularly."

"They needed a clean canvas, April. There was a degree of deliberate accuracy from what I see." Her words seemed cold and clinical.

April watched the screen with interest as Dr Pritchett moved away from the head to something that had caught her attention. She lifted the victim's left hand and inspected the area just above the thumb. The intense light from above seemed to bounce off the whiteness of the skin. She called for Hannah who moved swiftly to her left before pointing the camera lens directly at the indicated area. April could not help but lean forward.

***

Bennett sat at his desk and looked at the notes he had made. Nothing seemed to make any sense. One story tells of a happy marriage, a marriage that stood the test of time even though a child had been born and from what he could understand, fostered or adopted but as far as people were aware they, as a couple, did not parent the child. A kind and charitable man who was heard to shout, shout when he was apparently alone in the house. When his wife was alive, they heard nothing. He tossed his glasses onto the jotter pad on his desk and rubbed his forehead.

"At whom would you shout if alone? Why would you shout at no one? For what possible reason, apart from the odd expletive?"

He checked the file he had requested on both Philip and Patricia. Spencer had retired at or around the age of sixty-five after working as a sales representative for a firm based in Harrogate. It involved regular travelling, and in some cases, time spent away from home. He had taken up charitable work shortly after that. Patricia had worked part-time in local schools and also in the library one day a week as a volunteer. He thumbed through, searching for a reference to a child but he found none. He turned to the computer and investigated 'children's homes'. There were quite a few in Harrogate: some were for the disabled and one, St George's House, was specifically for police officers' children, those who have lost one or both parents.

There was a tap on the door. Owen filled the space.

"Did you know there was an orphanage in Harrogate for coppers' kids?" Cyril muttered whilst looking over his glasses.

Owen shook his head.

There was a long pause as Cyril looked again at his notes. "I'm puzzled, Owen, by some info I received earlier. Tell me, do you ever shout when you're alone?" Cyril turned and watched Owen approach.

Owen thought for a moment. "Maybe when I'm driving. I'm alone then but I often shout at some other inconsiderate road user. I admonish myself sometimes too but I wouldn't say I do it when there isn't just cause." Owen looked at Cyril for some reassurance that he did the same. "I suppose I do come to think of it."

Cyril raised his eyebrows surprised at Owen's use of the word 'admonish'. Dictionary for breakfast, Owen?"

"Shreddies, same as Spiderman. Compulsory in our house at the moment, sir."

Cyril immediately regretted his question and put his hand to his forehead. "Sorry, where were we?"

"Do I shout when I'm alone, sir, I think you asked? I said I did."

"Right! You do, you ... admonish yourself either when in the car or not?"

"Yes. Why?"

"There's a report that Spencer could be heard shouting

when he was at home but the couple next door believe he was alone. It was as if he were shouting at someone. They hadn't seen anyone enter nor had they seen anyone leave. According to them, and they've lived there a long time, it has only happened since the death of his wife." Cyril steepled his fingers and placed them beneath his chin.

"It was definitely him?" Owen asked, leaning on the back of the chair positioned in front of Cyril's desk.

"They mentioned on some occasions it didn't seem to be his voice but that was not often."

"Losing a loved one can have some strange effects on people, especially if they've been together a long time. Maybe he's just angry and that's the way he gets it out of his system. A mate of mine lost his father unexpectedly and it came as a great shock. He couldn't handle it. He would go into the woods alone and shout his dad's name over and over again at the top of his voice."

Cyril looked down as if comprehending.

"Why mention the orphanage?" Owen folded his arms; he had been lucky in his early life as his grandparents had brought him up, otherwise he might have gone down that same route.

"According to the neighbours, they had a child, no, she had a child, a boy, before they met and it was given up. Children's home probably and then adoption. I'm assuming he was born in the late sixties or seventies, so he'll be in his fifties if he's still alive. If adopted they more than likely had a change of name too. If those dates are right, it would make Patricia eighteen or nineteen when she had him. What makes a mother give away a child, Owen?"

Owen said nothing but felt as though he could suddenly

crumble. If he knew that, he might not have felt a degree of guilt all of his life as if it were his fault his family had failed. He shook his head. "I've no idea, sir, sorry." He swallowed hard, feeling hot and uncomfortable. "The child is better in a home where they are cared for and loved than with parents who resent their very existence."

"True, Owen." Cyril frowned and let Owen's words of truth sink in.

"I take it you've never heard of mother and baby homes? Unmarried mothers were sent there by their parents who were afraid of the stigma of illegitimacy irrespective of the welfare of the expectant mother. From what I know and that's not much, they were not pleasant places at all. The daughter was sent away from home during the pregnancy too to make sure nobody found out. Did you want me, sir?" Owen had had enough of this conversation and felt decidedly uncomfortable.

"Yes, sorry. The search with a cadaver dog and detectorists needs doing and as soon as possible. We have pressure from above to move swiftly with this case. Can you sanction it?"

"I'm sure I can if we have to get the construction moving." Owen smiled as he had already set the wheels in motion.

As Owen left, Cyril picked up the phone. "I need information on a Fraser Melling, born possibly early seventies. No exact date. There may well not be a birth certificate owing to the circumstances of the birth. Investigate children's homes or mother and baby homes in Bradford, Leeds and then Harrogate and the surrounds. Check to see if he shows on any of our police records.

Check Inland Revenue, National Insurance and importantly NHS for the number too, as soon as, please. I also want a warrant to search and take any relevant evidence from Spencer's address."

***

Dr Pritchett spoke whilst still looking at the hand. "Something's been written here but it wasn't done today, neither was it yesterday considering the way certain parts have been removed through washing and rubbing. We may be able to enhance what we have once it's digitally enlarged."

"Could it be the same ink as on the forehead?" April sensed a degree of excitement build in her stomach.

"It looks like a blue-black pigment, maybe ball point pen, but we'll know after tests. If I were to guess, he has jotted a note to himself so whether that will be relevant is questionable but we'll keep all our options open." She looked up towards April. "We've all done it, grabbed a pen and scribbled. We then hope it's not indelible!"

***

The warrant had come through quickly. Cyril was back at Spencer's address. He went straight to the framed photographs positioned on the sideboard. Something had nagged at him but he could not put his finger on it until he had been told of the possibility of the birth of a child.

The photograph seemed faded but it was still clear enough to see the face of the person. Removing his phone, he captured the image before enlarging it on his screen. Glancing at another framed photograph of Philip and Patricia's wedding, it confirmed the woman was indeed Patricia, but taken a number of years before their wedding. Looking back at the early photograph he was surprised to see where it had been taken.

Chapter 8

April sat looking at the whiteboard. There was a growing degree of noise from the staff now working within the Incident Room. Each person, each activity added to the room's ambience. The frozen faces of the two victims stared back at her, photographs copied from those found in their homes; neither was current. *Say cheese* came into her mind as both were smiling, the smiles that are held for those brief moments when the camera points and time is captured forever.

Opening the file detailing Betty Cole's autopsy, she looked to see if there were any other similarities in the two cases other than the head trauma and markings to the face suffered by both victims. There was nothing. Picking up the phone she dialled Dr Pritchett. It was answered immediately.

"Julie, it's April."

"I'm just finalising the details of Spencer's autopsy. It will be a while yet."

"I'm ringing about Betty Cole, I just wondered if there were any other similarities other than the type of weapon, the stamp and the forehead printing?"

"I didn't do that autopsy, neither have I had time to review the findings in any detail." She paused waiting for April to continue, there was definitely an agenda, a suspicion and curiosity that had brought about the call.

"I feel foolish asking but ... she didn't have any writing on her hand, did she? There's no mention within the report."

"Isaac and his team wouldn't have missed it."

Dr Isaac Caner was a Home Office pathologist of long-standing and yet Julie's curiosity was now piqued.

"What if it were very, very faint?" April's question seemed wrapped in uncertainty.

"Very, very faint. The body is still here. Give me fifteen minutes and I'll get back to you but I think you'll be disappointed, April."

April's stomach fluttered, was she grasping at straws? She scanned the reports from the two people who had discovered the bodies. One had called from a landline, the other a mobile. *Did Spencer have a landline?* she thought turning to her colleagues in the room. "How many people here have a landline?" Only one person of the group waved a finger.

It was as she had assumed, these phones and the telephone directories that went with them, had gone or were disappearing owing to the convenience of the mobile. However, both victims had lived in their respective homes a number of years, they were both of a certain age. April recalled her grandmother and remembered how her phone was not only a convenience but a lifeline. Staring at the phone on the desk, a landline, she picked up the receiver and called Cyril, wondering if the very fact they still had what appeared to be old technology at a modern police station reflected the state of the present-day Force.

"Bennett." His telephone manner was never welcoming.

"It's April. Do you recall seeing a landline in Spencer's house?"

There was a pause. "I'm here now. Usually they're situated in the hall but I'll have a check."

April could hear the movement and then a faint siren from an emergency vehicle off in the distance.

"There's a phone socket in the hall and there's a line coming to the house from a pole just across the street. There's no phone and no modem either. We know he had a mobile and that's with the technical chaps to check the phone and call history but I'm not holding our breath as there's quite a backlog."

"You are in a queue and we'll get to you as soon as possible!" April imitated the automated voice one often heard when put on hold.

Cyril laughed instinctively. "Indeed, April. However, I know it's not a smart phone so we're only talking numbers so that may jump it up the list."

April's mobile rang. "As if by magic ... I'll get back to you in a minute. That will be your good lady wife ringing me."

Cyril said nothing but hung up.

"April, I've given both hands a thorough inspection and there's nothing, sorry." Julie heard a faint sigh of disappointment.

"I just had a feeling – Thank you, sorry to cause you—"

"No trouble. Looking for links. Always worth checking. Things have been missed in the past. Never stop asking."

Cyril answered straight away when she called back and listened as April explained the reason for her call to Julie.

"Good policing, April. Never leave anything to chance."

"One other thing. You were at Cole's house, sir. Where was the phone?"

"In the hallway near the front door. On a telephone table, it had a chair attached. Very sixties. Why the fascination?"

"If I called you and you needed to jot something down, important info, what might you do?"

"Grab a pen and—"

"You've no paper." April leaned forward anticipating the answer.

"Jot it on my hand whilst balancing the phone against my shoulder usually. If I had a pound, for every time I've done that!"

"Do you recall if there was a notepad near Cole's phone?"

Cyril laughed. "Ask me one about sport! Not a clue. Look at the CSI 360 degree video of the house and rooms, a trick we learned from estate agents. It gives an impression of how the house was found before anything was moved. Now you can help me. I'm going to send you a photograph. Can you identify the building in the background? Call me back if you know."

Within minutes the image was received. She called Cyril. "It's the old Ripon Teacher Training College, apartments now, I believe."

"That's what I thought but when this was taken it was still the Teacher Training College. The photograph shows Patricia Spencer but she wasn't married then, she was Patricia Melling. I'm guessing, 1971 or '72. We've discovered at that time she lived in Bradford and not

Ripon." He paused allowing April to digest the information. "So why is she in Ripon and why is she photographed alone in front of the college? The more important question is, by whom?"

"Had she gone for an interview? Could this be taken at the time potential students came to look round after applying or before? We know she worked in schools as well as the library, so did she attend and did she qualify as a teacher?" April asked.

There was a pause. "That should be easy to find out. Let me know the answer when you know." Cyril was quick to delegate.

"Sir, I'd really like you to collect any pens, ball point pens, found at Spencer's house. Something was scribbled on his hand and I need to know if he wrote it and, if he did, try to match the ink. I'll check also for any pens at the charity shop he might have used. It will give us a clue as to the place he made the jotting on his hand."

"Any pen I see here I'll mark a piece of paper so the ink can be checked. Couldn't whoever have killed him have written on his hand and left the pen?"

"According to scientific evidence it wasn't written the day he died."

"I'll do what I can April."

April immediately arranged for Brian Smirthwaite to visit the charity shop and question those there. She knew from his expression the request was not to his liking.

"They always seem to smell the same," Brian grumbled as he stood. "Thanks!"

"You have to take the rough with the smooth, Brian. The next time we make enquiries at Betty's I'll make sure you volunteer."

"As if that will ever happen in my lifetime!"

"We need a sample of Spencer's handwriting and hopefully Sonya might be back but if not, we'll need to interview her so get contact details. I also want ink samples from any pens they've been using, scribble each on a piece of paper, that should be ample for Forensics." She knew the thin layer chromatography would take time.

Brian brought his hand to his forehead as if making a cheeky salute. Turning to the computer April tapped in her password and the North Yorkshire Police logo disappeared.

Within minutes she had found the file for which she searched. Cole's house was certainly impressive. She skipped through the images of various rooms until she found the hall. As she had hoped, the video clearly showed a notepad next to the telephone. She stood and went to the whiteboards. Fortunately, there was still a police presence at the house. News of the death of a wealthy spinster would attract the wrong attention and the valuable home would make an easy target until any relatives could be contacted or security organised. She needed to take a much closer look at the notepad.

***

The PCSO was present as April parked the car on the double yellow lines that ran down sections of Duchy Road. She paused and looked along the road at the parts of the large houses she could see peeking from above naked winter trees and shrubs. There was a maturity to the gardens, a grandeur to not only the general houses, but in the traditional architectural style even down to the gateposts, these often being marked with the names of the homes. Many houses on the road had been converted into apartments but those that remained in single occupancy seemed to hold an attraction of their own. Cole's, was such a house.

The gravel on the driveway crunched beneath her feet as she admired the surroundings. The façade, clearly visible from the road, seemed to glow in the light of the winter day; the curtains were open. The PCSO unlocked the front door. The warmth struck April as she entered and a smell reminiscent of wax polish and lavender quickly assaulted her nostrils. The light penetrated deeply into the hallway and onto the stairs as she paused. She slipped on a pair of gloves.

The telephone table was there immediately to her right, a piece of furniture from the sixties and clearly an anachronism when considering the other furnishings and the general ambience of the house. She admired the avocado-coloured telephone and smiled. Her grandmother had owned the exact same model. The notepad was there, the top page folded back. Collecting it she moved to the light. The upper page contained a number of doodles They were mainly patterns but one circle split with a curved line separating black from white was identifiable. Most were mindless scribbles drawn whilst the person chatted or the caller waited. Lifting the pad, she noted one of the pages below had been removed, torn, leaving an irregularity to the perforations. She felt a flush in her stomach. Holding the blank page at an angle, the impressions became visible, regular corrugations left after someone had written on the page above, the missing page. At this moment she could neither discern the words nor even the letters but she knew Forensics could. For some inexplicable reason she took out her phone and photographed the first page, the page of doodles.

She needed permission to remove the item and after a quick call, the pad was safely added to the card lined envelope she had brought to protect the pad from further damage. The time, date and place were added to the evidence.

***

The charity shop was quiet as DC Brian Smirthwaite entered. The light tinkle of a bell summoned one of the assistants from the room at the back. The aroma in the shop was as he had predicted; they seemed to have a smell all of their own whether it be from the numerous racks of clothing or from the items that could not be cleaned, he could never determine. All he knew was that he found it unpleasant. He showed his warrant card. The forced smile he gave to the assistant was not reciprocated.

"My colleague spoke with an officer already but I suppose you want to talk to me. I was with Philip that day. Sonya, I'm Sonya. They said you'd be back." Sonya put her head in her hands. "He was ..." she blew her nose on a handkerchief quickly retrieved from her cardigan sleeve. "Such a kind soul. It's a cruel world and I'm glad I'm not young again."

"My condolences, Sonya. Everyone we've spoken to has told of his generous character."

"I saw there's another one, another murder, the MBE lady, Miss Cole. Harrogate was such a genteel place, Mr?"

"DC Smirthwaite. And it still is and that's because of caring people like yourselves."

"She came in here, that lady who was also killed. She dropped items off." She blew her nose again before steadying herself on the counter. "I'm alright. How may I help?"

Within thirty minutes Brian left the shop. The cold air seemed suddenly clean and fresh and he inhaled deeply.

***

Cyril checked the whiteboards on entering the Incident Room. There was an industrial buzz about the place, it was an atmosphere that excited him, as if the wheels of the investigation were beginning to move at a greater pace. The information he had requested had already been attached. Patricia Melling had attended Ripon Teacher Training College starting in the September of 1971. Studying English and History, with a specific focus on Primary Education. She left in the spring of '72 after the first induction course observation within a school in Bedale. *'At the request of the student. (Personal reasons)'* was all that was written detailing the reason she had left. Checking the file, he found details of her birth certificate. Born April 10th 1953. It showed the names of her parents and their occupations.

Shakti came into the room and tossed her coat over the chair. "We've only the one person by the name of Fraser Melling and born 1972. However, we have a few of that name born around the time and living in West Yorkshire. Our nearest match does not show on any records to be living at the family address. I've checked the electoral rolls and it shows only Patricia and her parents. No siblings and there's no mention of Fraser. We've completed the usual background checks to trace him but there's a blank there too from 1973. It's as if he just vanished."

Cyril turned a chair and straddled it.

Shakti continued. "That's not unusual if he were removed from the young mother within days of her giving birth. Mother and children's homes did not have a good reputation. Did you know there were five-hundred thousand kids taken from unmarried mothers from the 1940s to the 1970s and one hundred and eighty-five thousand of those mothers were believed to have been forced to give up their child. I would imagine that was down to social pressure, stigma and maybe even as it meant another mouth to feed. Fascinating, sir, yet at the same time it made upsetting reading. Did you know there were such things as Moral Welfare Officers linked with unmarried, pregnant girls?" She did not wait for Cyril to answer but saw him shake his head. "No, I didn't either. They merged with social workers in the seventies but the title sounds so clinical, cruel and Victorian."

"Possibly Dickensian," Cyril managed to say before she continued, with anger still evident in her voice.

"So, the child would be removed from the mother just like that. I've read a report where they refused to allow a mother to see her newborn baby and yet they extracted her milk. Who the hell would do things like that and who could possibly believe it was right? Those, they say, were the good old days and yet we're talking of the seventies!"

Cyril shared her anger and could see the anguish on Shakti's face. "The child would become untraceable from that point onward. Fostered and then adopted, the mother and child link permanently eradicated, probably in the belief it was best for the child." Cyril took a deep breath. "And yet we read of occasions where adopted children have found their birth mothers many years afterwards."

"More than likely due to the support of the people who adopted them. Without that help, where would a child start? They'd have to know they'd been adopted in the first instance and I'm sure many didn't until much later in life, if ever at all." Shakti tossed her notebook onto the desk and folded her arms as if to lock out any further discussion.

Chapter 9

Owen watched as Dr Green arranged one of the bones a millimetre closer to the next. It was precise to the extent it made Owen think of a grand master deliberating the move of a priceless chess piece at a critical moment in the game. Green was immaculately dressed, the most outlandish checked rust-coloured woollen jacket over a dark-grey shirt. The bow tie, obviously hand tied, was a contrast of stripes of various subtle hues. The clothing combination would, on many men, clash and look possibly foppish but on Dr Green it seemed stylish and fitting.

Green saw Owen cast an eye on his attire. "Dare to be different, Detective Inspector, my mother preached. I've always loved clothes, they're a weakness, especially bow ties. Now, I digress. Part of the sternum, the breast bone. We're missing some ribs, a femur for Jacqueline here and various smaller bones from the wrists and ankles which I doubt we'll ever find; there are twenty-seven in the hand alone but then you'll be aware of that. However, you can see she retains much of her head. Charles over yonder, is not as complete." He moved across to the other table. "A greater number of bones are missing and many have been damaged under the tracks of the machinery. I can say for certain the damage to the scapula I mentioned at the discovery site was done post-mortem."

Owen leaned over the remains as Green picked up the bone. He was initially uncertain as to how they knew whose bones belonged to whom. "Does that mean—"

"Charles here was in the ground when the blade struck the body. We believe it to be a trenching tool, a spade or shovel, but interestingly one with a semi-curved blade. Turning he collected a folding camping spade. "Similar to this. You can see the curvature closely resembles the damage to the bone."

"Is that the only damage?" Owen handled the object, running his finger along the blade edge.

"You were there. You saw the way the site had been excavated in the most brutal way. Many of the bones have been fractured and crushed but we have enough. I can give you approximate ages, too. Charles here was about twenty-three and Jacqueline was younger, maybe nineteen."

"Why those names?" Owen moved back to the first table.

"JCB, the bulldozer that discovered them. Had we found a third body we had a letter spare."

"Right! DNA?"

"ASAP. Sorry, messing." Green chuckled. "It pays to try to have a sense of humour when working with the dead. We've used a relatively new procedure, one created to help identify bodies caught in natural and man-made disasters. It speeds the process and is equally as accurate. DNA profiling from bones can be a time-consuming process as I'm sure you know. Generally, the best profiling results are obtained using demineralization protocols that aim to dissolve fully the bone matrix to release the DNA. However, we can now use a rapid, semi-automated DNA extraction method based on partial demineralization. DNA is extracted from finely ground bone powder. Manual handling is minimal and the extraction process is automated as soon as the samples are loaded on a Promega Maxwell FSC instrument." Green could see Owen losing interest. "Sorry, I do get carried away. Science and technology move on at an incredible pace and I find it so fascinating."

"How long will DNA stay in the bones?" He picked up Jacqueline's skull.

"Amazing the condition considering the circumstances. DNA has been extracted from a Neanderthal bone seventy thousand years old. However, quality DNA? Up to one hundred and fifty years should not be a problem and the extraction techniques are improving all the time."

"And we have their DNA?"

Green smiled. "We do. We know roughly the length of time they've been in the ground too and if we have knowledge of those who went missing at or about that time period you should, with the co-operation of relatives of the missing, be able to effect a match. You might want to know that we also discovered some canvas and brass buckles. We think they are part of a rucksack. That might suggest they were, as we initially believed, hitch-hikers or should we say, one may have been. I believe a further search with dogs and detectorists is imminent?"

"Tomorrow for two days and if nothing further is discovered the site will be handed back to the construction team."

"Will you be present, Detective Inspector? I would be happy to come along."

Owen thought of Job and those who did not bring comfort and smiled. "Indeed, I shall. Firstly, we will need to get the ball rolling, trying to find a match between these bones and the people to whom they once belonged."

***

April and Smirthwaite looked at the ink samples, trapped in a transparent forensic bag, he had collected on a single sheet of paper from the charity shop. There were a number of colours and types of ink.

"They had a bloody jam jar full of pens. She watched me mark the paper with each bloody one before bringing a pen from under the counter and telling me that it was his favourite." He shook his head and exhaled demonstrating his frustration. "I'm sure she did it deliberately! I hate those shops!"

April giggled. "I doubt that, she just followed your request. To begin with, did you ask if he had a pen he preferred to use?"

"Never thought. Anyway, she did give me this. It's like a diary of the days when he was working, detailing briefly the staff and any problems with the shop and customers. It also included a list of any donations from those who came in off the street. He'd have made a good doctor as his handwriting looks like some kind of cursive Russian script! However, if you screw your eyes tightly and hold the pages away it becomes magically legible. I spent a bit of time with it and made a fascinating discovery."

"I'm all ears, Brian."

"As I said, he always noted those making charitable donations – for reasons his colleagues could not understand. We have three separate occasions where donations were left in the last month from the same person … Betty Cole MBE. Here, then here and the day before she was killed … and just before he was too! Note, he also added 'MBE' after her name on each occasion so it's clear that he knew her and of her title."

"Is there any significance other than she deposited some items in a charity shop? Am I missing something?" April looked at the notebook and held it away from her face.

Brian shrugged his shoulders. "No idea but as it might prove to be a piece of the jigsaw at some stage in this investigation it's worth making a note of. Anything back from Forensics?" He handed April the notebook.

April flicked through the pages quickly. She stopped before turning them back one by one. In the top corner and drawn faintly in pencil was a stick man and in the subsequent pages similar sketches appeared but each time the figure had been changed. As she flicked the pages one after the other, it appeared as if the figure moved. He seemed to fall and then slowly disappear.

"Have you seen this, Brian?" April flicked the pages again.

"Flip-book cartoons. We used to make those at school. I hadn't seen it. Good though. If you check, there's a symbol or shape further towards the back."

She turned more pages until she discovered a small drawing of a circle divided by a curved line drawn on a loose leaf trapped between the pages. She felt a faint chill on her neck but at that moment said nothing, giving herself a little more time to digest what she had just observed.

April picked up a Post-it note. "Finger prints found on the bottle used on Cole are mainly hers but there's another clear set. We took Crookson's prints as he was there the morning after the murder and his prints are on the bottle. It's difficult to determine at this stage who held the bottle last and there's some smudging which suggests a gloved hand may well have also held it. As she doesn't have a carer it's likely to be those of the murderer."

"And Spencer?" Brian propped his backside on the edge of the table.

"Predominantly his, but again, there's evidence that it was held by someone wearing gloves. What's clever, Brian, in these instances, is they know the wearer was using the same type of latex glove. Glove impressions can be either two or three dimensional as we know, depending on the type of surface they've touched or held. Finding the make of glove and tracking that to the killer would be like finding one prawn from all the rest in the Atlantic but what we do discover is the size and shape of the hand. It also tells Forensics about the hand used, whether left or right, therefore we should know their dominant hand although the evidence from the bottle strike is fairly conclusive."

"What did we do before Forensics?"

"Often, we didn't, we guessed. There's strong evidence to suggest the person wearing the gloves was male owing to the size of the glove." April waved her open hand. "Whilst you're here and we're talking pens and such, I found this on the notepad left on Cole's telephone stand. It's gone for investigation for second page writing, indent writing." She retrieved a copy of the photograph she had taken of the doodles.

"I'm always doing that, doodling when on the phone, but usually only at work. The other times I'm on my mobile so I tend not to have the long conversations."

That made April pause. He was right. She too only doodled when the phone was attached, rarely when she was on her mobile and usually when on hold and listening to indifferent wallpaper music.

"Did you know you could use a soft pencil as they do on the telly and that would show if something was written beneath? Doodling's instinctive and comes from within, helps you focus the mind." He paused and cocked his head. "That's yin and—" He didn't complete the sentence but pointed to one doodle and then the notebook. "Is the inner hippy in me coming out, not that I recall flower power but my mother would like to believe she was a child of the sixties but she's too young. It's the music that attracts her." He sat back as if reminiscing. "Flower power! Christ, we need some more of that."

"Yes, it made me stop on seeing that, Brian. Can the Supreme Ultimate or the taiji, Brian, a kind of Chinese philosophy, on this occasion be a coincidence? Black and white, day and night, positive and negative … peace brother!" She stuck two fingers in the air. "We'll have to see."

There was a long pause as both realised the significance.

April broke the silence. "As a matter of fact, Brian, the old pencil trick is the best way to destroy the evidence but you knew that—"

Brian just frowned, concern clearly written on his face. "I'm going to pay another visit to Spencer's house. Wish me luck. I wonder if any more similarities will appear."

***

The house seemed eerily quiet as he pulled up outside. He waited in the car for a while and contemplated the coincidence of the symbol. He then thought of the cartoon. A PCSO tapped on the window.

Brian showed his ID and moved towards the door of the house.

Smirthwaite had searched houses belonging to the deceased before and it never seemed to grow any easier. Standing in the hall he quickly felt the chill emphasised by the clear sense of neglect. Any house left empty in the middle of winter soon seemed inhospitable.

Brian stood momentarily as he looked at the drooping flowers within the vase on the sideboard, the water green and almost opaque due to the length of time it had sat there. *Men and flowers seemed a contradiction but at least, he'd made an effort,* Brian thought. He lifted the glass vase and held it towards the light of the window. The green water had the appearance of what he believed primordial soup might look like. He pulled a face. Beneath the round, crochet doily on which the vase had sat he noticed a small card trapped beneath. He removed it.

Happy Christmas, Mummy.

Turning the card in his hand he frowned before reading

it again. The handwriting seemed immature and clumsy. He photographed it and slipped the card back beneath the vase.

***

The A59 was deserted, the ribbon of tarmac stretched as far as the eye could see. Only the farmer whose property was up and to the left of the valley was allowed to use the road. The white covering of snow settled on the higher ground, seeming to reflect the sun on the occasions it broke from the grey and mottled overcast sky, bringing an unnatural brightness and sharp-edged shadows to the scene.

Owen and Dr Green watched as the dog moved with fluidity and grace over the churned yet frozen ground, an agility that contradicted the difficulty posed by the ground's conditions. It moved backwards and forwards as if uncertain of where it wanted to be but the energetic movement of its tail showed its eager determination; it was clearly a game and a game it must win. At first, the dog kept returning to its handler who rubbed its chest and sent it away again. Within five minutes the dog sat.

"He's found something." The handler stumbled across the terrain shouting words of encouragement as the dog stood, its whole body swaying as the handler approached. "Good boy! Well done!"

Owen and Green followed, moving as quickly as possible to the position. The dog was rewarded and slipped back onto the leash. The CSI officer also joined them and within minutes the soil was carefully fractured and turned over, revealing a softer sub-layer that was swiftly removed.

"It's part of a femur," Green said as he rotated it in his gloved hand. "Probably the missing one." Further excavation brought the other part of the damaged bone. It too was removed. The bone's location was added to the gridding system. "In this instance it would be sensible to use what3words to identify the approximate location but protocol is protocol. I'll use both."

The dog was released to run again. At the furthest extreme of the area, it indicated another find. It sat eager for its handler to come and investigate. On the surface there was nothing but as soon as the top covering of frost-hardened ground was removed, the broken cranium was revealed.

"That's it with this dog for today. Considering the false scents, the clumps of rotting wood and roots, the old fella's done well." The handler rubbed the dog's ears. "There may be more to be discovered but that's for tomorrow."

Owen looked at Green. The forensics' team immediately set up a tent, lights and started to dig. The dwindling daylight was not on their side but the immediate area needed digging. Within thirty minutes further bones were found as well as fabric, leather and some metallic items.

"Looking at these, Detective Inspector, I believe we have another body."

"Bob or Belinda?" Owen asked without taking his eyes from the bones laid on the tarpaulin.

"Sorry?"

"JCB." Owen turned and faced Green.

The penny eventually dropped and Green smiled. "One

or the other. I'll let you know when I find out."

Considering it was now early evening, the return to Harrogate along the A59 seemed particularly bright owing to the moon clearing the cloud and reflecting on what remained of the snow. The white domes, the 'golf balls' of RAF Menwith Hill, seemed bigger and more threatening as he approached and Owen wondered, as he had done on many occasions, what secrets they held. However, now he needed to call in at the Little Ale House, grab a swift pint and then home. Glancing at the dashboard clock he realised his little Spiderman would be in bed otherwise the beer would wait.

Chapter 10

King's Road was busy with evening traffic; it was one of the main routes out of the town leading from the centre towards Bilton and Skipton Road. A gritting wagon, bright yellow with flashing warning lights, spread salt across the carriageway. The fine particles shimmered almost jewel-like as they skipped across the wet surface. More snow had been forecast. It was a steady walk from the Harrogate Convention Centre owing to the continuous incline. As the day had ended and the light died, the temperature had fallen well below freezing. After fifteen minutes, hands were retrieved from deep within the coat pockets and with the help of a street light the address, written on the back of a hand, was clear to see.

Turning left at the row of terraced houses, their dark stone walls were set well back from the pavement and separated by short gardens. Privet hedges formed a green, frosty fence to many. These houses to the front, however, were not the destination; the lane running along the back of the properties was closer to the target. That lane allowed access to the house on Dixon Terrace. The time was now just after seven. A black cat walked along a low wall and paused before jumping into one of the gardens.

The latch on the gate made a noise louder than expected but the sound was quickly lost. There was no light in the back room, the kitchen, of the house. Listening with an ear close to the glass panel on the door the television could be heard. The brown grab handle positioned vertically on the stonework next to the door confirmed it to be the correct address. A gloved hand slipped onto the door handle but it did not move. Standing back, eyes scanned the darkness to the right of the door. The key safe was there where it had been spotted earlier in the day. It would take only minutes to open. The four numbered dials would soon give up their treasure as the pick slid quickly into the side of each. Patiently, the latex gloved hand rotated each dial until the key safe 'gate' was located. Combinations were usually a relevant date, something easy to remember or a year or a combination of the day and month of birth. This one was more naïve – 4,3,2,1. The small block switch was pulled down and the key safe opened.

***

Ralph, April's rescued Great Dane, had decided he had chased enough balls for one cold morning and the lamp post at the intersection of two paths was of greater interest. April sat on the bench and pulled the coat more tightly round her frame. The morning sky was streaked with orange and a fine blanket of mist lingered low just above the tree tops. She had adopted the dog after its owner had been murdered in bizarre circumstances and even though Owen considered it more donkey than dog, she had rescued him and he had soon become a loyal companion. In some ways their meeting had been a saviour for them both. Within the hour she would be at work.

As April walked past Owen's desk, he informed her of the discovery of the remains of the third body.

"That dog was amazing and so was the handler." His enthusiasm was clearly evident. "So many distracting scents. It kept beavering away and it found more remains very late in the day." Owen's mood immediately changed. "Unfortunately, there may be more, we'll have to wait and see. That's all we need, April, to find a bloody serial killer who's been on the loose for fifty years." The earlier enthusiasm appeared to be quickly waning.

"That's one way of looking at it, remember, after that length of time they might also be dead or they could have been put inside for another murder and these have just never been discovered until now."

Owen sat back. "Great minds. Dr Green's theory is similar, he said the perpetrator might well now be dead and his guilt could well have died with him."

"You could be chasing a ghost, Owen. Good luck with that! You'll need a Ouija board!" She frowned and moved away.

On logging on to her computer, April immediately noticed the forensic report detailing the findings on tests performed on Cole's notepad, was now on file. She quickly opened the document. The images of four pages had been processed and positioned in order within the file. The written content was visible on the polymer film on which the image had been fixed after being identified using electro-static detection apparatus. That process had allowed for a more thorough look at not only the first page after the missing sheet, but also down to the fourth page. There was obviously repetition and the marks grew weaker the more pages viewed.

It was the second page that made April pause. Forensics had identified and highlighted something that had been written at an oblique angle. The accompanying notes suggested it was not an indent from the above or missing page and was probably written on paper inserted within the pad at some time when it was open. It was also, according to the opinion of the handwriting analyst, written by a different hand than the rest identifiable on the other pages.

The letters, *Bl   H – s,* were all that could be seen; the last letter after the 's' could not be determined but it was evident one was marked there. It was printed rather than written in cursive script and the analyst believed the author to be right-handed. There was clear evidence to suggest the words were scribbled in haste using a soft-pointed implement, maybe a mechanical type drawing pencil. On close inspection, April could see the marks indented from the previous pages making it difficult, even under a loupe, to determine each letter. It had taken a professional eye to discover the letters highlighted.

Also attached to the file was the ink analysis taken from the pens collected from the shop and Spencer's home. There was a match with the ink sample remaining on the skin of his hand; it had come from his favoured pen. April contacted Brian Smirthwaite and passed on the information. Within five minutes he sat opposite.

"Have they managed to trace what was scribbled?" Brian's tone was eager and excited.

"As yet, no. I believe they're utilising a kind of digital ultraviolet process but the end result takes time. From what you discovered we know Spencer had met Cole at the shop. For some reason there was a symbol found on the pad and within his notes which might be relevant. We're keeping an open mind. Do we know if they were associated in any other way, other charity connections maybe? As yet, that's a blank too. However, it appears Cole has a niece living in France, she's coming over with her partner to sort the house and her aunt's estate. Cole's younger sister passed away a few years ago. The likelihood is, the niece will inherit everything unless, of course, it's been willed to charity."

Brian sighed. "It wouldn't be the first time, neither will it be the last. She couldn't have been murdered for—" He stopped himself saying what he felt as it sounded foolish knowing they had another similar murder and he had no known relatives as far as they were aware.

"It crossed my mind briefly, Brian. I've had a chat with Mary Bailey, the said niece, and although she spent a lot of time with her aunt when she was younger, since moving abroad after she married a few years ago, they only communicate on the phone. She spoke fondly of her and seemed genuinely upset."

"I could call on the neighbour, he may have seen the press pictures of Spencer and may well have seen him at her house."

"Do that and take some additional photographs, maybe take one of him with Patricia. Just a hunch." She glanced at the time on the computer screen. It was just after ten. The morning had started positively.

Brian stood. "Did you see the findings from Spencer's house? The card positioned beneath the flowers came as a bit of a shock considering she's not seen her child nor, as far as we know, had other children. We're checking if the flowers were delivered from a local florist. There are no business details on the card and they've been there for quite a while considering the condition of the flowers, as well as the card, suggesting it could be old."

April nodded. "Nothing has been tracked so far and that's strange. I've asked Forensics to check the handwriting against what we have so far and the possible age of the ink."

***

Cyril sat on the edge of Owen's desk as they discussed the human remains found the previous day. Owen swung back and swivelled on the chair, his legs barely missing the desk.

"I was telling April earlier, amazing that cadaver dog. It never bloody stopped. The handler believes they've covered over eighty percent of the planned search area and the detectorists should sweep the site by late afternoon. Stuart Park is there and I know Dr Green was keen to see it through to the end. He'll ring if they find more. I was talking with Hannah last night and she said she could imagine all the wooded waste land beside the roads throughout the UK that never sees footfall from one year to the next, could be hiding similar secrets and when you consider the number of people who go missing annually, she could just have a point." He shrugged his shoulders. "And that's before you consider that bodies might have been cut into bits and spread around, just tossed from cars and wagons."

Cyril waited patiently for him to finish his hypothesis before removing his handkerchief. He blew his nose. "Hannah's a fitting example of a Job's comforter, Owen. Let's just concentrate on what we have before we disappear up our own backsides worrying about what might be out there."

Owen stopped swivelling as he saw April rush into the area. She pointed instinctively at them both.

"We have another murder." She sounded breathless and concerned.

Cyril stood and turned towards her.

"Male. Found this morning. All the hallmarks including the stupid postage stamp. Head injury similar to those suffered by Cole and Spencer. Initial report from the primary responders reveals the house was not broken into. Front door was locked but the back door was open, wide open when they arrived. The victim was last seen yesterday afternoon coming home from a meeting of the British Legion. His name is Stanley Meredith, known to all as Stan. All the same hallmarks with the same consequences."

Cyril turned to look at Owen and then back at April. "Who found him?"

"A neighbour who parks his van at the back of his own home which overlooks the rear yard of Stan Meredith's house. As with the milk man and Spencer, he saw the open door and with the temperature being well below freezing he thought he should check. He'd picked him up the evening before on his way up King's Road, that's how we know where he'd been."

"Doctor? CSI?" Cyril was already heading towards his

office as April followed.

"There now as we speak and he's been certified dead at the scene."

"Get your coat." Cyril was already taking his off the hanger.

***

April parked halfway down Bilton Drive. A number of marked police cars were visible alongside the CSI van. Blue and white tape was stretched tightly across the narrow entrance to De Ferrieres Avenue that separated the houses on King's Road and those on Dixon Terrace. The PCSO was positioned just beside the wall. A number of people, some of whom Cyril assumed would be from the Press, had collected and were eager to discover the reason for the police activity.

Bennett showed his ID.

"Just up on the right. We've sealed off Dixon Terrace as instructed and house to house enquiries have commenced." He pointed to the police vehicles. The officer was clearly enthusiastic. "Quiet area this, normally."

"You know the procedure with the public and the Press?"

The officer nodded before lifting his shoulders as if trying to protect his ears from the cold.

"The public might have information and you are the front line. If they do, take contact details if they mention anything, no matter how insignificant you might think it to be and report it immediately."

"Sir." He turned and smiled at April before lifting the

tape.

Once signed in, the CSM gave Cyril more details before they moved to the back door of the house. April immediately noticed the grab handle. She nudged Cyril's arm and pointed towards it. Cyril continued to focus his attention on the key safe to the side of the door. It was closed and still looked to be locked as he manoeuvred across the yard on the step plates to take a closer look.

"With a bit of practice and pieces of an old drink's can they're easy to open." The CSM spoke with a degree of authority. "Providing they have time, that is and it's not too dark."

Cyril looked at him and then at the safe. "Really!"

"If you check on YouTube it shows you how!" The CSM pointed to the open door.

The room was bright as the LED lamps flooded the confined space. The curtains in the living room were drawn closed. To Cyril's surprise, the body was still in the chair facing the television screen, head back, mouth agape.

One of the CSI lifted a bottle with the same care as if it were a bomb, to preserve any evidence. "The doctor believed he was killed before midnight but he couldn't be more accurate until the post-mortem."

Glancing round the room, the walls held a number of photographs of men in uniform. There was a dagger, a Fairbairn-Sykes pattern fighting knife, mounted on a wooden stand alongside a winged horse cap badge.

"Commando?" Cyril muttered under his breath as if unsure if the man in the chair, his face towards the ceiling, could at one stage in his life have filled that role. Only time would reveal the truth.

***

Richard Forsyth sat in the kitchen of his house clutching a mug of tea. Cyril and April sat opposite. April judged him to be about forty.

"Goodness, I've known the old chap years. He lived there when we moved here in 2010. He was very kind, sometimes looked after the kids if the missus had to nip out. He was in the Falklands, although looking at him now, you wouldn't think he'd have the strength to pull a clucking hen off her nest. He told the story of his war exploits so often he could put you to sleep."

Cyril smiled more from sympathy than amusement. "It meant a lot to many. Their life in some cases. Lest we should forget." Cyril spoke with a degree of reverence.

"If you've never been to war, I don't believe you can fully comprehend the effect it has on a young man, particularly at the age some were. I remember my dad telling me about Granddad fighting during the Battle of the Bulge." He paused, looking at both April and Cyril. "Sorry. Anyway, after the forces he was in a number of jobs, caretaker in schools and stuff. If he wasn't looking after the country, it was people or buildings. A caring man you might say."

Cyril frowned, looked at April and then checked his notes. Meredith was seventy-four years old. He jotted a quick note to himself. "I believe you gave him a lift last night?"

Forsyth nodded. "He was coming up King's Road. He always wore a fluorescent vest sporting a red poppy over his overcoat. 'No good living through war and being hit by a

57 bus.' he would always say. He'd been to his beloved British Legion. He must have raised thousands in the time he's been involved with the charity. I've heard it's closing down at its present site so what he'll do then is ..." He stopped realising what he had said.

It was the word 'charity' that made April turn to look at Cyril. It had not gone unnoticed.

"I'm sorry to sound daft but I didn't understand the stamp," Andrew pointed to his forehead. "Stuck here and then there was some writing too. I didn't look too closely, didn't touch anything. I just dashed out and phoned. You know, at first I thought he was sleeping but when I touched his shoulder his head fell to one side and it was then I saw the blood. His eyes just stared at the ceiling. Frightened the bloody life out of me I can tell you."

"You didn't touch anything other than his shoulder?" Cyril queried whilst wondering what else had been touched.

"Sorry, yes, but nothing else. As I say, I thought he'd dozed off with the telly on."

"Did you see anyone unusual around here yesterday evening?"

"I came out after my tea to check the van was secure, it's a bit dark as there's only two street lights and they're the new energy saving things which are as good as a glow worm's arse. Stan's kitchen light was on and I could see him at the sink. The door was closed. He's usually on the ball with security."

"Did he have a key safe?"

"Aye, he does, and I have the combination, just in case. I've used it once or twice when he was out shopping and called the wife to say he thought he'd left the stove on. He hadn't. I fixed it there for him."

"And was the door wide open this morning?"

"Yes, at about seven to seven fifteen and it was absolutely freezing. I could see the flicker of the telly as the door inside, the kitchen door, was open too. Why would someone kill such a lovely old chap? And, more importantly, for what? As far I we knew he had nothing to speak of and glancing round, nothing had been touched. Even his prized possession, the knife, was still there and they're worth a bob or two I'm told."

Cyril's mobile rang. He left the room as he answered it.

"No more remains but the detectorists have made some interesting finds. I'm releasing the land back to the builders so the work can continue." Owen sounded relieved.

Cyril quickly returned to the kitchen. "Mr Forsyth, there's a grab handle by the back door. Was he infirm? You mentioned about his strength earlier."

"Not really, a while back he had an accident. He has a motorbike and sidecar. Had it years but for some reason it tipped over when he was cornering on one of the country lanes and he broke his leg quite badly. He went to stay with his sister in York until he was fit enough to be on his own. He was never married from all accounts, and she died last year. She'd suffered a number of strokes. I fitted those when he came back home; there's one on the front door too. Once the leg healed, he didn't need them but told me he'd leave them up as they might come in handy one day, as he wasn't getting any younger. Still has a slight limp. His sister's passing hit him real hard. There was no one else apart from a nephew he hasn't seen in years. He referred to him as a 'useless no-mark'. Used his mother, always on the scrounge. Stan thought he was into drugs, the heavy stuff, but as long as he didn't bother him ..."

April made a note to check.

"The bike?" Cyril quizzed. "Could that be the reason for the attack?"

Forsyth shook his head. "Still in the shed, I checked. You can see through the net curtains if you know how. It was never fully repaired. Sidecar was a real mess and parts of that were scrapped. I think the accident frightened him and what with his sister's passing, he never really got back into his full swing. I know there's been a couple more murders recently a woman who was awarded an MBE and another elderly Harrogate resident. The stamp and the writing, is that significant?"

Cyril looked at April and back at Forsyth. "At this stage of the investigation we'd be grateful if you can keep what you saw confidential. It might just be the key to tracking the killer."

Forsyth nodded. "Yes, not a word. Let's hope you find the bastard before—"

Cyril and April stood, bringing an abrupt interruption to his growing anger. "We're grateful. If you remember anything else you can contact me on this number at any time." He handed Forsyth a card.

Chapter 11

The briefing had been hastily convened. A number of officers positioned themselves around the room and the usual buzz of conversation was broken by the occasional outburst of laughter, brought on by someone cracking a joke. The blue glow from the large wall-mounted screen tinged the whiteboards. Some officers were familiarising themselves with the latest information which had been added to the boards as Cyril and Owen entered. The conversation quickly faded.

"Thanks, I know this meeting was called at short notice but there's a need to get our ducks in a row. We may be looking for two killers, serial killers, one from the present and maybe, one from the past. Owen." Cyril turned to Owen as he sat down and folded his arms.

The blue of the screen turned to black before a coloured aerial image of the A59 at Blubberhouses appeared. People leaned forward instinctively and the noise of the chatter rose significantly.

Owen raised a hand and the noise died.

"We definitely have the remains of three people, one male and two female. The images changed as he shared the information about the discoveries. Any skeletal damage you might see is, I'm assured, done post death and we now know the bodies were buried in shallow graves, maybe just scraped over. Further tests will take place to ascertain the cause of death in each case. There were also the remains of two sheep found close by, mixed with the remains. Few bones remained as it's believed they had been dispersed once the flesh and fleece had gone. Dr Green, the anthropologist working alongside the forensic team, believes they'd been placed there within the same time frame and may well have been left as a distraction, deliberately placed above the shallow graves. Anyone wandering into the area and smelling the decomposition would put it down to the dead animal. Owing to the location, it's highly doubtful the area saw much footfall. Having now identified the DNA of two of the victims and knowing their approximate ages, we're searching for the relatives of the known missing persons of the period where we have a possible match. That, I've been informed, is more difficult than it would appear."

Owen turned to look at the screen as he pressed the remote control and another image flashed up. "This is the remains of a purse found at the scene and you can see it has obviously been in the ground some years. It contains coins. The newest coin is a fifty pence piece dated 1973, but there are also some pre-decimal coins. Remember ..." He looked down at his notes. "Decimalisation came into being on the 15th February 1971 and some coins from before that date were still legal tender. However, you can see from this image the purse contains a farthing, which was discontinued in 1961, as well as a half-crown. That was discontinued in 1969."

DC Colin Forbes, one of the new officers present, waved a hand. "I still keep an 1847 Indian one cent piece in my wallet but I'm not that old. It's a lucky charm. Could those out-of-date coins have a similar significance. The year they were minted, maybe?"

Owen turned and scrutinised the image. "Like a birth date?"

Forbes nodded. "That was what I was thinking, yes."

Owen nodded. "Thanks, Colin, we'll make a note of that. Other metallic objects and cloth remnants are now being analysed in the hope further clues will be revealed and the owners identified." Owen glanced at Cyril and sat down.

"Thanks, Owen. The site has been handed back to the developers. However, we have a forensic archaeologist assigned to them until completion, should they discover anything else."

April stood. The screen cleared and she went through the information she had, focusing predominantly on the latest murder of Stanley Meredith. The victim's military career had now been established. Cyril had been concerned that he had been too old to have fought in the Falklands conflict but checking the ages of the two hundred and fifty-five British personnel killed in the action, he had quickly changed his mind and the historical army records corroborated Meredith's involvement. On leaving the forces he had taken a number of jobs, predominantly as a caretaker in schools. His last position was in a care home. It was noted his final two appointments, which spanned nine years, checked out and he left with excellent references. Since then, he had been involved in a voluntary capacity with the British Legion.

After an extensive discussion, she was about to sit down when the door opened. Brian Smirthwaite entered and he moved quickly towards April.

"Crookson knew Spencer." He spoke quietly but excitedly.

"Tell, Brian. This is for you all." April watched as he retrieved his notepad.

"I've just been to see Rodney Crookson, Betty Cole's neighbour and the man who found her body. To be honest, he made out he didn't know Spencer initially. I showed this photograph to his wife, Jennifer. She'd seen him on more than a few occasions going to and coming from Cole's. Crookson then recalled seeing him in the house. He couldn't recall why he'd gone round. He'd popped in unannounced and Cole and Spencer were having tea. They were introduced but he said he could remember neither his name nor the exact date it occurred."

"Did he know why he was there?"

Brian shook his head. "No, but Jennifer Crookson suggested it might have been to do with organising a charity event. She said she vaguely recalled it was something to do with a reunion of some kind but she couldn't be sure. It was a few months back, possibly a year; maybe a school, college or something to do with the charities she supported."

April turned immediately to look at Cyril before focusing her attention once more on Brian. "Brian, we have a new photograph of the latest murder victim. Pay the Crooksons another visit and see if they recall seeing him at the house. Shakti, I want you to call on the organisers of the Harrogate

Branch of the British Legion as soon as. The dots are slowly being drawn. All we have to do is join them in the correct order."

Her optimism was not conveyed to those in the room, particularly Brian, who did not relish his latest instruction.

***

Shakti pulled onto the parking bay in front of a large stone building which housed the Harrogate Victory branch of the Royal British Legion. Set along East Parade, the architectural style was imposing. It had been arranged for her to meet one of the members there. After the first fifteen minutes she knew she would learn little other than to consolidate the character reference they had received from Meredith's neighbours. According to the interviewee, Meredith had seemed his usual self and left after tidying the store cupboard. He was always keen to help at the centre as well as promote the charity and raise money; if anything, he seemed more ebullient after the Christmas period. The members had all been shocked and saddened on hearing the news of his death.

"I still can't quite believe it. To think he was here, where you now are, less than twenty-four hours ago. We just never know what the future holds."

Shakti realised she would get no more information. She stood and was about to leave. "Thank you. If there's—"

"There's one thing, Detective."

She could immediately tell from his troubled look he was unsure about passing on the information.

"It may be nothing but I thought about it yesterday, too.

When my wife and I were chatting with Stan, she noticed something. My wife's pretty astute, perceptive you might say and I've learned over the years to appreciate she sees changes in people, no matter how small or subtle they might be; a woman's intuition, maybe. Just before Christmas she asked me if there was anything wrong with Stan. When she met him at the festive bash, he didn't seem himself. When I asked what she'd seen, she told me she couldn't put her finger on it but asked me to keep an eye on him. 'Troubled' was the exact word she used. 'He seemed troubled and not the Stan she'd known for some time'. Do you know, she's not often wrong, my missus, when assessing folk."

Shakti sat back down but said nothing for a few moments. "Was that the last time your wife saw him, at the Christmas party?"

"No, now I come to think about it she was here three days ago when he came in. We normally hold our meetings on the last Thursday in the month but with Christmas, then New Year and with family commitments, our next meeting is only in late January. Give me a minute." He left the room.

Shakti could hear a telephone conversation outside in the corridor. He returned.

"According to Gwendoline, that's my wife, he popped in to collect something. She said he'd left a parcel, wrapped in brown paper. She was busy in the office. He popped his head round the door, collected the parcel and left. 'Abrupt' was the word she used."

"Troubled, abrupt. Doesn't sound like the same man we were talking about earlier."

Shakti could see the anguish on his face as if suddenly

he felt a degree of responsibility.

"I can honestly say I didn't see the difference in him, even yesterday. However, he was distraught at the news that this building was going to close, but alternative meeting arrangements have been made. He seemed fine with that decision. I suppose now we'll never know if something else was troubling him, will we, Detective Constable."

"Do you or your wife know what was in the parcel?"

"No, sorry. Never considered to ask."

"Was it addressed to him care of the Legion?"

"I couldn't say but I'll investigate."

Shakti smiled. "Investigate, yes."

***

On arriving at Crookson's house again, Brian Smirthwaite deliberately knocked on the front door with more force than usual, not exactly expecting a welcome.

"You again! Did you forget something?" Crookson blocked the doorway.

Brian removed his ID. "Murder enquiry, if you remember. Evidence is being discovered constantly and with that, we act upon it as soon as we can. If that's an inconvenience, I offer you an apology but then you'll have to accompany me to the station, and believe me, it's far more comfortable to chat here. Is Mrs Crookson in?"

Rodney frowned, the reluctance to comply clearly evident. He moved sideways, begrudgingly, allowing Brian to enter as he called out. "It's that police officer chap again, I'm afraid." He paused whilst taking a deep breath as if to calm himself. "You'd better go into the lounge and I'll see if

Jennifer's available. I have to protest and say I view this as harassment."

The atmosphere and the welcome of the previous visit had clearly evaporated; even the ticking of the grandfather clock in the far corner of the room seemed to grow louder the longer he waited.

"Sorry, old man, she was upstairs. She's coming now. How may we help this time?" The frustration in his voice was clearly evident but the animosity had been tamed.

Brian removed the photograph of Stan Meredith and placed it on the coffee table.

"Another? It's like a bloody who's who of Harrogate!" Rodney Crookson grumbled whilst picking up the photograph and withdrawing his glasses from behind the silk handkerchief lodged in the top pocket of his jacket. "Bloody hell, that's Meredith, Stanley Meredith if I'm not mistaken. Parachute regiment, or so he often said. Could have been a cook and bottle washer for all we knew. Falklands vet—" He paused and peered over his glasses, the reason for the unexpected visit was now dawning.

"The latest victim, Mr Crookson. It appears you knew all three. You didn't kill them, did you by any chance?" Brian never let his face slip but he knew his words would not be dissimilar to lighting the blue touch paper on a large firework. He was right in his assumption.

"How dare you, sir! I, I ..."

"Just requires a yes or no answer and then we can move on, Mr Crookson."

Crookson had turned a deep shade of crimson and minute beads of white spittle were ejected from the corners of his mouth as he protested further. "Move bloody on? I will move on, sir. I play golf with your commissioner, I'll have you know, and I can assure you that I'll be having words. Your insinuation is not only rude and ill-founded, it's slander. I'm not surprised in the least that the police receive little to no help from the man in the street these days if this is the way you conduct yourselves ... jumping to silly and unfounded conclusions."

Jennifer Crookson entered the room and her presence seemed to defuse the situation even though she seemed more flustered than ever. She immediately looked at her husband with concern and then at Smirthwaite. "Is something the matter?" She moved and stood next to Rodney, slipping her arm in his in a show of solidarity.

Crookson removed her arm and slipped his around her shoulders, drawing her closer. "I'm saddened to say there's been another killing, darling. It's Stan Meredith." The anger was still clear in his voice.

Jennifer brought her hands to her face. The shock conveyed was immediate and sincere. It took a moment for her to regain her composure. "He knew Betty very well. She was very supportive of the Victory Branch of the Legion. Her father, Squadron Leader Sir Henry, was ever present and involved with a few veterans' charities and when he passed away, Betty continued with the family commitment. She always laid a wreath at the Cenotaph every November."

"The keystone to the killings seems to be Betty Cole. Do you know if they were acquainted outside the charity circle?" Brian looked now towards Jennifer.

Jennifer perched on a chair arm and shook her head whilst glancing at Stan's photograph. Rodney sat down too.

"I know she was a governor in a number of schools over the years. She was once a key figure in a home of some kind in Richmond as was Stanley but that closed and he worked in schools. They knew each other but to what extent I couldn't honestly say, but there was also a strong link with the Forces. She knew the other chap from the charity shop but if they had other connections, I'm afraid I'm unaware of them, I'm sorry. What's distressing is that each and every one of them, Betty, the other chap and Stan seemed to be kind and gave of their time freely. Goodness, Betty received her MBE for her charitable endeavours. So why are they victims of such a dreadful crime? People seem so evil at times." She handed the photograph back to her husband as she waited for an answer to her impossible question.

Smirthwaite remained silent, giving Rodney Crookson ammunition and time to retaliate. He knew what was coming by the developing facial contortions that were forming alongside the colouring of his cheeks.

"I really don't know what the world's coming to. You people are never seen patrolling the streets anymore, knife crime and drugs seem to be the main news stories. The police seem to do nothing apart from ingratiating themselves with various people in marches, prancing, dancing and waving rainbow bloody banners. You can't even remove those parasites sitting and blocking the streets when honest, hard-working folk are trying to get to work. I've seen it on there." He pointed to the television. "It's happening far too often whilst you're travelling round in rainbow decorated cars, fining people for speeding and parking offences. When will you return to old fashioned policing methods? When will you sort the wrong from right like in the old days? Bring back local police stations rather than sticking them miles from anywhere, way out of town and whilst you're at it, bring back the birch. Deal firmly with the disrespectful little shi—" Jennifer squeezed his leg. "Sorry, darling. The whole thing is out of control."

Smirthwaite continued to remain silent, knowing anything he should say about modern policing methods would fall on deaf ears.

"So, who will be next, me?" Crookson tossed the photograph back onto the table. "Now, if there's nothing else, we'd like to be left in peace, if that's at all possible in this town. You're supposed to protect us, not pester us!"

Jennifer rested her hand on his and turned towards Brian. "As you can well imagine, it's been an upsetting couple of days and your visit has done nothing for my husband's blood pressure. Betty's death was bad enough but now this. I really don't understand."

Collecting the photograph Brian moved into the hall. He wanted to tell them just what the police had to do on the limited budget they received but knew it would be inappropriate. He had upset Crookson enough for one day.

Chapter 12

Cyril sat to the right. The room was filled with a number of chairs spread like a fan facing the rostrum. A Tennant's auction was always a pleasure to attend. The modern building, set to the edge of Leyburn, seemed to be more hotel than auction house. The modern stone edifice gave the appearance of an imposing country house. The interior was also deceptive with its sweeping staircase, café and restaurant. It was a far cry from the many auction houses he attended. Julie had enjoyed viewing the exhibits, particularly the 'Mouseman' furniture. Cyril marked his auction catalogue and as each lot was sold, he jotted down the starting price and the hammer price. He had seen a number of paintings he knew he could live with but he had come for only one, an oil painting depicting Bolton Castle in Wensleydale by Reginald Brundrit. Since seeing a painting by the artist hanging in the hallway of Betty Cole's house, he had recalled this one coming up for sale. He held open the catalogue; its estimate was low but he was wise enough to know that was to tempt the buyers.

"Will we be finding space for it or do you feel others will have the same idea as you?" Julie whispered as the auction continued.

Cyril had scribbled *Hammer £275 limit!!* on the catalogue page, adding the two exaggerated, oversized exclamation marks.

She took his pen. *You are buying dinner if you fail to get it for that,* she scribbled next to his price.

"Now on screen is Lot 76. An oil on canvas by Reginal Brundrit. A charming and perfectly sized painting conveying the tranquillity of the Yorkshire Dales. You can almost hear the skylarks." The auctioneer smiled. "I can start this straight away at three hundred and ten … twenty … thirty … forty pounds. I'll take fifty."

Julie blew in Cyril's ear. "Out of the water, Bennett." She watched as he closed the catalogue. A look of despondency on his face.

"Four hundred and seventy-five pounds for this charming oil for the final time." There was a pause before the hammer fell. "Sold to the internet."

"Bloody internet!" Cyril grumbled before rolling up the catalogue.

Julie and Cyril left the room.

"Italian food, I think." She linked his arm. "The one in Ripon. It's on our way."

Cyril chuckled. "That'll be nearly six-hundred quid with commission."

"You can't buy them all, Cyril, but today you weren't even close."

Cyril had been buying at auction for a number of years and was philosophical about the process. "Like buses, Julie, another will come along before the end of the year, you mark my words. Italian it shall be."

***

Owen had not been home long when his mobile rang. Christopher was tucked up on the settee in his pyjamas and was looking at a book Owen had been reading. It was Dr Green.

"Sorry to disturb you at home, Owen." The formality had been dropped after the third day of their acquaintance. "One of the detectorists came to the site to check the drift of soil moved into a large bank during the initial clearing. He discovered what he thought was a dog disc, but it was silver. On one side in worn script is engraved, *On no account must this person have horse serum*."

"What's that?" Owen asked whilst glancing down at Christopher who was still engrossed in the book.

"I'll not take your time now as I'm aware family time is most precious. However, I'll call in with more answers once I've completed my research. To me, it could well be a stepping stone in your investigation. Have a good evening and I'll check in with you tomorrow."

Owen's mind was now galloping, teased by the information Green had provided. *Did it belong to one of the victims and if so, what was horse serum?* Owen moved and Christopher's head slumped on the side of his lap. He was fast asleep.

Once the child was in bed, he googled *horse serum*. It looked more diverse than he had originally thought but it seemed to predominantly be used as an Anti-Tetanus Toxoid serum produced from horses. Some people were found to have a serious allergic reaction to it. Owen slipped the laptop onto his knee as he continued to read. He had received tetanus injections, not only as a child but as an adult and knew little of the vaccine administered or what tetanus was. Reading the facts was engrossing. Tetanus was also known as lockjaw owing to the fact that the body would go into severe spasm if untreated, to the extent bones could be broken. In the 1900s, tetanus killed 85% of those untreated. Now, human anti-tetanus immunoglobulin is used in place of horse serum.

Closing the computer, he looked across at Hannah who was sitting reading. 'The silver disc is of its time.' The thought conjured the image of more modern medical alerts carried by those in need. 'What if it did not belong to one of the victims but the killer? Would the killer know if it had been removed during a struggle? If they discovered it missing only later, would they risk returning – especially if the body had been buried?' He frowned but the thought of the conversation with Green filled him with excitement.

***

The Harrogate police station set out of town on Beckwith Head Road always seemed like a beacon of light on the dark winter mornings. The roadside row of leafless trees stood stark and outlined against the gloom of the sky. They seemed elegant yet ethereal in the streetlight's glow. People drifted in and out of the modern building as the shift changed. The sound of voices represented a new dawn chorus.

Brian stood in the kitchen area as he dunked a teabag into a mug of hot water. April leaned against the unit.

"The Crooksons knew all three victims. He suddenly jumped on his high horse too when I questioned him. I know it's unlike me, but I did feel a degree of empathy for them with me turning up like the proverbial bad penny a number of times. As his wife said, they'd had a few shocks in such a short space of time." Brian failed to express the full extent of his exchange. "I'm checking where Cole was a school governor and if there's a link with Meredith. I'm looking for this place in Richmond they mentioned." He tossed the teaspoon into the sink.

"Thanks, Brian. Let me know as soon as. Go back a few years and look for any connections with other institutions. Spinsters tended to fill their time with that sort of thing."

He left and April watched Cyril walk past the open door on his way to his office. She anticipated the 'T' sign formed with his two hands, signalling tea was required but none came. He seemed deep in thought. Returning to her desk, she glanced at the computer and noted a file had just arrived. It was further details from Forensics concerning the notepad found at Cole's house.

'We have every reason to believe the words on the note are, *Black House*. There is something else noted below the wording but again it is more difficult to interpret. We can offer an informed guess. It may well be either the number *72 or 73*. It is also believed the note was written after the doodles were scribbled on the upper page and this will clearly be significant in determining a time scale.'

"Black House." April said the words out loud. She

printed the information before moving through to the Incident Room. Picking up a pen, she added the information to the side of the photographs showing the different pages of the notepad.

"I've heard of the Red House but not the black," Harry Nixon chipped in whilst holding a mug of coffee. "It's now a retirement home in Ripon but at one time it was a children's home."

April turned, a look of curiosity was clearly etched on her face. "Ripon?"

"Yes, it's in Ripon. I only know because my aunt went to view one of the apartments. Beautiful, I believe. I heard she's going to commit. It's the security that attracts her to the place even though she's not that old."

April moved to one of the desks and logged on to the computer. Within seconds the search was done. "It was opened in 1946. A Dr Barnado's Home on Palace Road, Ripon, catering for children between the ages of two and five. Probably a private home before that. Once there, these kids would be fostered or adopted, I guess."

"The new development has been built throughout the entire grounds." Nixon leaned over her shoulder. "Hard to believe it was once a home for kids."

"Changed in 1975, taking children with learning difficulties. Closed in the eighties. But this is not the Black House, Harry."

Harry Nixon put down his mug and moved to the board before tapping a finger on Patricia Spencer's photograph. "When did she have the child? Where is she on this photograph? Why attend college for such a short time? The house you're looking at is what ... a mile from where she's standing, less as the crow flies? Remember, at that time, unmarried mothers didn't have any options and children would be easily lost in the system of secrecy. I doubt you'd be able to trace those who were 'given up for adoption' I believe the term was. I'm sure there's a closure period of one hundred years for records identifying individuals. Even if you tracked down the child, once they're of a certain age, they would easily disappear."

"They should still have a National Health number and they'll still hold valuable DNA." April sounded more uncertain than ever. "That's if we get even close to tracking them. Right at this minute, we need to focus on a different colour, Harry."

"The National Health number will mean nothing as it will be attached to a person we will never discover unless, of course, the true mother and child were reintroduced and the mother knew the child's new name and identity. It's happened I suppose."

***

Cyril stared at the computer screen as Owen pulled up a chair.

"We have a positive DNA match for two of the three found near Kex Gill. One male, one female. Peter Naylor and Sarah Parker-Jones. We have concluded that, despite the damage to the skulls, both were killed by a blow to the head. From the evidence it was initially thought from a strike by something like a ball pein hammer. I take it you're familiar?" As soon as he said it, Owen knew he had made a mistake.

Cyril immediately turned to Owen with a clear look of disdain. "Before you were born, Owen."

"Sorry, yes. They couldn't be sure but what Dr Green did say was that whatever did hit the skull was a concentrated blow executed with some force."

"Rock in a sock," Cyril mumbled as he turned back to look at the images on screen. "Go on."

"Naylor was twenty-two and Parker-Jones nineteen. They went missing two months apart. What's interesting is the evidence suggests she went missing first but her disappearance was not reported for quite some time. Apparently, she just took off, didn't even inform her employer. It was only after her parents contacted the hotel where she worked to say they'd not heard from her did the report go out. No mobile phones, internet or CCTV then of cou—" The more he tried to explain his thinking, the more he felt as though he were treading on eggshells. "Her parents lived in Lytham. So, as far as I'm aware there's no direct route other than taking a number of trains or buses or both."

"Then, in the seventies, it was easier to hitch a ride," Cyril offered.

"The parents offered a reward but nothing transpired, nobody came forward other than a few crank calls. They had some guy who said he could find the missing if given a piece of their clothing but as far as we know he wasn't approached. Why is it those missing often attract the strangest of people and dubious eyewitness accounts? It's still the same today. Peter Naylor was different as he'd planned to travel. He'd booked time off work, walking and camping in the Lakes. Again, no one knew where he was, where he'd planned to be. It was only when he didn't return to work after the holiday did alarm bells ring. He could have been dead ten to twelve days before anyone knew."

"Both were found next to the route they would have used if we accept that she was going home and hitching a lift and he did the same heading to the Lake District. I take it the DNA is matched to surviving relatives?"

"Yes, siblings as in both cases the parents are dead."

Cyril shook his head. "And they never knew the truth about what happened to their children. Even though I have no kids, it doesn't take a great deal of imagination to comprehend the emotional rollercoaster and trauma involved in such a tragedy. There would always be that hope they might come home, walk through the door or be found."

His words made Owen think immediately of Patricia Spencer. "Maybe even worse for Spencer's wife who had to give up her baby. I don't know which could be more traumatic."

"I take it, Owen, you've considered they might have been killed by Sutcliffe, the Yorkshire Ripper? The dates would work and the use of a hammer would fit."

"Thought he was later?" Owen frowned realising this was always a possibility. "Earlier you mumbled something about a rock."

"Catalogue of bloody police errors, that, when you look into it but you have to remember, as you did earlier, it was of its time. The police, us, were still using card index and we produced so many the floor of the room holding them had to be reinforced allegedly. No computers like we have today. I believe that case was the justification for the development of HOLMES, mind you, that only came fully functional around 2004. HOLMES II, followed, an administrative support system that was primarily designed to assist senior investigating officers in their management of the complexity of tracking serious crime but as I always say, if you put crap in, you'll get crap out. Supposition too was a weakness; only sex workers or those women staying out late at night could possibly be victims so it was like the hounds were chasing a false trail."

"All hit with a hammer and cut with knives and screwdrivers?" Owen's voice faltered as if he were seeking confirmation.

"Rock in a sock was one attack. The victim survived and didn't press charges. That was about 1969 but the majority of his crimes were later. We or should I say they, the officers, subsequently believed there were more cases left undiscovered and, as Hannah remarked to you, many could be hidden just like these. He drove the roads, probably picked up hitch-hikers. He killed because he was on a 'divine mission' so I guess these people could be easy targets."

"I thought all of his victims were women?" Owen perched himself on the corner of a desk. "Or am I doing what they did in the past, jumping to conclusions? The fact is they discovered a dead male."

"There were plenty of men found murdered and I say with head wounds too but they wouldn't fit the pattern they believed Sutcliffe was following."

"Keep an open mind." Owen chanted Cyril's mantra.

Cyril raised a finger. "Indeed. Work from evidence no matter how insubstantial that might be. Sutcliffe will have travelled the A59 on many occasions and could have taken any opportunity given to him."

"I need to talk with Dr Green about rocks in socks being a possibility," Owen mumbled.

"The third victim?" Cyril moved to the whiteboard to inspect the photograph depicting an array of bones placed roughly to form a skeleton.

"Hard to believe they once walked and breathed."

Chapter 13

Shakti Misra was staring at the latest information deduced from the notepad found on Cole's telephone table. She had noted the link with the similar symbol found in Spencer's notes. Removing a sheet of A4 from the desk, she started to add the letters that were clear, beneath which she wrote the word 'Black' ensuring it contained the correct upper-case letter. There was definitely an 'l' after the 'B'. The list of potential words started to grow: Blank, Blade, Blame, Blood, Bleak, Bleed, Blaze. Before running out of ideas, she added Blimey!!

Sitting back, she read through the list underlining the word 'Blood' for no other reason than it had an affinity with 'Black'. It was then she circled 'Bleak'. Bleak House. She immediately recognised it as the title of the work by Charles Dickens but she had never read it and knew nothing about the story nor the characters. However, adding the word to 'House' certainly suggested an overall air of mystery in the process. It was only then, as April passed, did she feel as though she were wasting her time.

April stopped. "You look either puzzled or guilty, Shak. Are you okay?"

Shakti shook her head, laughing lightly as if embarrassed, but it was loud enough to be heard. Turning the sheet of paper round to face April, she explained. "There seemed to be a degree of uncertainty in the forensic report on the hidden text so I had a quick brainstorm of words that might be inserted in place of the word 'Black'."

April scanned the list and pointed to the word circled.

"It certainly sounds sinister enough, Shak. Have you read it?"

"I've never read any of his works but I've seen Oliver Twist." Shakti again sounded embarrassed. "'Kes', is the one book I remember from school. I'm not a great reader and I loved the film too." The memory evinced a smile.

April tapped the paper and a puzzled look flashed across her face. "Godparent, guardian and there's an issue with handwriting within the tale .... Nobody ... Nemo and a pauper. It's a complicated novel and possibly the first real piece of crime fiction as well as being an indictment that society is rotten to the core. You haven't wasted any time, Shak. I need to do some reading." She winked and tapped the paper with her finger.

Cyril came in holding the cup and saucer. The flowers decorating the fine china seemed a contradiction to the dark Yorkshire brew it contained. "Tell me what we know about Philp Spencer's career. I know he travelled and was in sales but with whom and what did he tour the country selling?" He took a sip from the cup. Shakti was waiting for his little finger to jut out at an angle but she was disappointed.

"He was a sales rep for Robert Hirst's." She checked to see if she could see any glimmer of recognition but there was none so she felt safe to continue. "They manufactured kids' coats, gaberdine with a winter lining, school uniform for many kids in the sixties and seventies but the firm was taken over by Carrington Viyella in about 1977. They continued to produce garments and he stayed with the company even though the head office moved away from Harrogate. Hirst's head office was on Hookstone Avenue and is now the Business Centre. They had a place in Bradford and both the buildings in Harrogate and Bradford had the same name, Hammerain House. I'm uncertain as to the reason."

Cyril scribbled the name and quickly moved on. "In 1971 he'd have been what? 22?" Cyril asked as April checked the details on the board.

"Yes, born in 49. He was 75 when he was murdered."

"A young man, a company car, expenses and travelling from the base here in Harrogate to all corners of the UK." Cyril took another sip.

"Their key manufacturing sites, of which there were about three, were mainly situated in the north east at Langley Moor near—"

"County Durham," Cyril interrupted whilst raising an eyebrow.

"It was called *Dryway*. He would have travelled there on occasion, maybe for samples and if he were visiting outlets in the area. Another couple of sites were in the Team Valley …" She waited but nothing came. "Gateshead. There was also Bradford as mentioned."

"Is that where he met his future wife?" Cyril tapped the pencil against his lips before slipping it behind his ear.

April just raised her shoulders. "They married in

Harrogate Registry Office in 1974."

"If you consider the case of the bodies discovered next to the A59, then our man here was in the perfect position to carry out the killings. Ripon had loads of students at the time, as did Harrogate and with the hospitality business being a major employer in the town, it was a magnet for young people from Leeds and Bradford eager to find employment. The problem is ..."

"Why would he? He's soon to be happily married with a nice home and a good job," Shakti added.

"So was Peter Sutcliffe. No, I paused because ..." He drank what was left in his cup. "I paused because I broke one of my main rules regarding supposition. Everything should be evidence-based but I can't help but wonder ..."

***

Green stood in front of the three skulls, each was labelled with a number of small, coloured adhesive circles. "The colours identify each individual. I've considered the possibility of the victims being initially rendered defenceless with some kind of cudgel, as you say, Owen, a rock in a sock. The evidence for such a strike is very real on the first." He held up what remained of the skull, turning it to the side. "You can see here a clear depression with radiating bone fractures. This was a heavy blow with a hard and irregular surface which could clearly come from a trapped medium sized stone swung with force."

Owen leaned forward and inspected the damage.

"Now if you look at this one and the other, the damage is of a deeper depression which, we believe, was caused by a pein type hammer. The centre of the depression would have struck the inner soft tissue and those shattered pieces of the cranium would have remained in place until the soft tissue was either consumed or eroded. However, it's the regularity of these indentations that gives us a clear indication of the weapon." He placed the skull down and collected a number of clinical reference photographs taken of other skulls damaged in a similar way.

"I see." Owen stood back. "These two could have been caused using the same hammer or weapon."

Green smiled. "The second body, that of Peter Naylor. If you recall, we believe Parker-Jones was killed first but then we must remember we cannot be fully accurate concerning the order of deaths."

Owen frowned as his statement seemed to contradict what he was saying. "Naylor was killed second but then you're unsure?"

"Nothing is certain with bodies that have been in the ground for so long. Let's just say there's a professional assumption. Don't you ever have those, a gut feeling based on experience and what evidence you have?"

Owen imagined reporting that to Cyril. He knew what his answer would be only too well.

"We can cautiously assume his killing was not fully planned, maybe we can say it was an opportunistic killing, if he even meant to kill him at all. We also have nothing to suggest he was killed at the location in which he was found ... Nor the others for that matter. We would normally look at other forensic evidence, pollen for example, but you saw the damage done at the site. I'll leave you, Owen, to conjecture the might haves and the maybes. In my mind, he was struck there, in that place. All I'm saying is we can never be one hundred percent sure."

"Is there anything from the metal and fabric found?" Owen had hoped for clarity and not greater opacity.

"Indeed. Come with me."

Green moved to the far end of the room and slid open a large, flat, tray-like drawer.

"We've tried to put them into categories, items we feel live together. This fabric is part of a rucksack, ex-military and probably purchased from an army surplus store. In the sixties and seventies those stores were in every large town and city. You could buy almost anything from radios, rucksacks to hobnail boots. This piece of fabric is probably part of a belt, maybe from an overcoat, possibly a child's overcoat. The buckle has remained although it is extensively corroded, as are the eyelets at the other end."

"Do you know the type of material?" Owen suddenly felt a flush of excitement.

"Gaberdine. Overcoat material. We found no other trace. This has lasted owing to its construction and waterproof qualities."

"So had it been attached to the coat there would have been a greater amount of material found?"

"Without a doubt." Dr Green adjusted his glasses as he pointed to the tray. "The ribbon-like material was heavily stained and fragmented, the colour possibly a navy blue. I know what you're thinking."

"Could it have been used as a garrotte?"

***

Cyril's phone rang. "Bennett." He waited as the caller was put through and he found himself doodling on the edge of the paper before him.

"DCI Bennett? This is Sonya."

Cyril thought for a moment. "Sorry. Who?"

"Sonya, you know, Sonya who worked with Philip at the charity shop."

"Philip Spencer?" Cyril brought a hand to his forehead and breathed deeply.

"Philip, yes. We didn't meet, it was another nice man." She sounded flustered and anxious. "He gave me this number and your name."

"How may I help, Sonya."

"The man said that if I thought of anything no matter how irrelevant I thought it might be I should call the number on the card and ask for a DCI Bennett. Is that you?"

"Yes, thank you for taking the trouble to call. Go on, please."

"Well, we were chatting in the shop and we talked about Philip. We were asked by the officer if he had any hobbies but your mind clouds over at times like that and especially at our age. Anyway, one of the girls remembered a customer who told us that Philip liked stamps and he did." She paused as if to gain breath.

"Stamps?" Cyril was slowly losing the will to continue.

"Yes, stamps, you know postage ones. If any stamps came into the shop, he would be the first to inspect them. We once got a full album and he advised us where to get the best price for them. His favourites, I seemed to recall, were the black and the red ones. To think it only cost a penny to send a letter back then. Not like tod—"

"Thank you very much, Sonya. That information is very important. We may need to chat with you again." He was just about to end the conversation. "Sonya, do you remember the name of the man who reminded you about the stamps?"

"It was Joe. He comes in to get clothes. I believe he's a rough sleeper. I once saw him in the doorway just near our shop but when they're wrapped up in a bundle it's difficult to identify them. He popped in regularly for clothes but we've not seen him for a while. We try to be charitable."

Cyril remembered noticing the jumble of items in the shop doorway after he had visited the shop. "Do you have any other name?" Cyril asked, his interest now even keener.

"I don't even know if that's his real name but he answers to it."

"Do you remember the last time you saw him? Is he always in the same place?" Cyril heard her chatting to someone who was with her, he assumed a colleague.

"According to the ladies, they said he came in the day before Philip died and he's not been in since."

"Thank you, Sonya. As I said, we may be in touch again."

"Nice chatting, Inspector Bennett." She hung up.

With his elbows on the table, he rested his head in his hands. Were these snippets of information a coincidence, an irrelevance or were they vital links for which they had been waiting?

Cyril moved through to April's desk. She quickly located the copy of Spencer's notes, now digitally copied. He felt it unlikely that someone coming into the shop requesting charity would donate but he had to rule out the possibility. She went through to the last page containing his notes. There was the name 'Joe' after which Philip had written – 'An envelope containing foreign stamps'.

Chapter 14

April and Brian Smirthwaite sat opposite Cyril in the Incident Room, now a hive of activity. The meeting had been planned in the hope of tying up some loose ends.

"This quick briefing is to find out why we're not further ahead. Information as well as forensic evidence is coming in, albeit slowly. So, where are we?" There was a pause. "April?"

"We now know that the writing on Spencer's hand was a note, it's probable he wrote it. Much of the evidence suggests this and even though we are only eighty percent sure there's always the possibility it was not. His writing varies to such an extent ... you could see that from the book Brian received from the charity shop ... Forensics believe it's an address, it's just a number they can confirm with any degree of certainty, the number 4 and the last word is Crescent. It was very well rubbed and if I'm honest, I'm amazed they can suggest even that."

Brian broke in as Cyril jotted down a note.

"His phone record and that of the shop show he did speak with Betty Cole on five occasions prior to her death. The calls varied in length and came from his mobile and one from the phone in the charity shop. We know that she called him from her landline to his mobile. Spencer did have a fixed line too but it's no longer connected and we haven't found the actual phone in the house." Brian looked up from his notes.

"Could whoever have entered the house that day have removed the phone?" Cyril asked, a degree of uncertainty in his voice.

April looked at Brian and then back at Cyril. "Why would they do that? From our checks, the number was disconnected just after his wife died. The dates match."

"Anything else ... No? I want a time line for Philip and Patricia as soon as. Birth to death for each. I also want to find a dropout named Joe, he's in the notebook and saw Spencer on the day he died. According to the shop assistant he dosses in the town centre. I want all patrols informed and we need a quick response. We have a pathology report on Philip and I want medical records for both husband and wife. Philip's will have been released for the autopsy. Are the blood results in?"

April shook her head. "As you know, they take time, unfortunately."

"There's something not right about this. We now have evidence to suggest one of those murdered was into stamps, not necessarily a true philatelist but he had an interest and the significance of that slaps me in the face but then what's the relevance with Cole and Meredith?" Cyril paused. "Indeed, so the clues are clearly of value. More importantly, I was told black and red stamps were a favourite of his." There was a pause where the background noise seemed to dominate the room.

"The Black House, Penny Black and the children's home in Ripon was called the Red House but then, sir, we cannot be sure that it was the word 'Black' written on the note. Shakti came up with the word 'Bleak'." April chipped in.

"Dickens!" Cyril whispered. "That's all we bloody need!"

"Yes, if you go down that specific rabbit hole there are some vague similarities linked to the author and a relevant and important piece of his writing, especially if we believe one of the characters was an orphan—"

Cyril held up his hand. "Sorry, I feel as though we're now looking to find links rather than investigating real evidence. Let's just keep to the facts."

April nodded.

"I want another sweep of Spencer's house with a focus for anything stamp related. Look for old letters, postcards. Anything."

***

The following morning Brian was back at Spencer's house. Shakti went in first. "I've searched Shak."

"Was it a man look, Brian?"

"Maybe. Christ there's something morbid about searching through dead folks' belongings." He stuffed his hands in his pockets. "I'm getting really cheesed off with all of this, Shak!"

She headed straight for the stairs. "You look again down here and then we'll swap. Move furniture, look behind pictures. Imagine you were hiding something you wanted nobody to find."

"Right." Brian's enthusiasm left much to be desired.

The rest of the search seemed fruitless until Shakti found the airing cupboard. The lagged water tank was cold. On a number of shelves were items of folded clothing. A fine film of dust had settled on the upper garments suggesting they had been there for some time. "Did you search the airing cupboard?" Her voice seemed to echo through the house.

"Just some neatly folded clothes, I think his wife's, dust and an old lagged water tank."

She lay on the floor and shone her torch along the off-cut of carpet allowing the light to penetrate the area beneath the lowest shelf, illuminating what appeared to be two shoe boxes stored at the very back and seemingly trapped by the shelf.

"Brian, I need your help." Shakti's voice carried a degree of excitement.

Within minutes the shelf and clothing had been removed.

"What do we have here?" Brian too suddenly found a new level of enthusiasm.

"Did you look in here?"

"Yes, but not as well as you, Shak, obviously." Both slipped on a second pair of gloves. He grinned removing the lid from the first box.

One of the shoe boxes contained a number of envelopes that had never been sent. Each contained the name 'Fraser' and was dated. They were in chronological order, all written in the same hand. Looking carefully at the dates, Shakti could see they were either penned in March or December. All were sealed. Bundles of ten were tied with a red piece of string and neatly stored within the box. The second box was full of stamps and postcards. The stamps had been roughly torn from envelopes and stashed in the box.

"Curiouser and curiouser!" Shakti said as she leaned back against the airing cupboard door.

***

April looked through the photographed copies of the items they had found.

"Love letters to a lost child. I feel quite voyeuristic reading these. In every case one was written around what we assume to be the time of the child's birthday, the other at Christmas every year from 1974 until the year before she passed away."

Brian responded. "The mental trauma might never go away and writing the short letters to the lost child might have helped her deal with the hurt and sense of loss. From what we know she functioned well and was considered a wonderful woman according to the people who knew her."

April quickly glanced at a photograph of one letter:

My darling boy,

I can see how big you are growing and to hear your laugh is just sweet music to my ears. I know you are being good for your mummy and daddy and I know they love you very much.
Be good and be kind.
X

April held the letter, her hand dithering slightly. She shook her head. "I find it strange she never signs the letters, just ends them with a kiss."

"Maybe that would be too painful," Brian answered.

April was immediately touched by Brian's sensitivity, it was seldom displayed, but maybe this case had touched a raw nerve as it had done with her.

"The other box was even more of a concern."

April held some photocopies of postcards retrieved from the box. Each A4 copy showed both sides of the cards. Brian picked up each in turn.

"Blackpool! Not been there for years. All I seem to remember was the cold, candyfloss, the amusements and the sea was a mucky grey colour. All addressed to Mr and Mrs Spencer."

"Bloody big tower?" April mumbled. "Remember that?"

"Yes, the tower but then once you've seen it you've seen it. Not exactly Paris by the sea. The piers too, I remember. Spent most of the time under those as it always seemed to be raining."

"What do you notice about the 'Wish you were here' notes?"

Brian checked each again in turn. "That's all it says and all signed with the letter F and x."

"All printed, block capitals."

"Who's FX?"

"I think the x symbolises a kiss, Brian. That leaves a letter F only."

"Fraser?" The name left Brian's lips slowly.

"That, Brian, we may never know but it seems logical."

"Blackpool, Saltburn, Bridlington, Whitby, Southport. All

seaside towns. All up north, as they say."

"Why do I have a nag that these were written by Philip Spencer himself?"

"You think he sent them? Why would he do that?"

"There's something about the print. We know his handwriting is difficult to read. What did you call it? Russian script?"

"Indeed. So, you believe he's printed these to conceal the fact he wrote them and yet he was one of the recipients. Why? To make it look more childlike?"

April raised her eyebrows. "That's why we're known as detectives. The plot thickens." She smiled as she put down the sheet of paper. "Maybe to placate."

Brian gave April a puzzled look.

***

The dashcam footage received after the appeal to the public was the first real visible evidence. It showed someone leaving the front gate of Spencer's house on Dragon Parade on the evening of his death. The time shown on the video was believed to be inaccurate as the owner was unsure how to set the time and date, but they were confident it was the same day and within the time frame requested by the police.

"This has been enhanced. We have a male, approximately five ten or eleven of above average build. Owing to the amount of clothing he was wearing to keep out the cold, we cannot see any distinguishing facial features. Gait analysis shows the person to be right dominant. There's no sign of a limp but the body posture suggests he is trying to keep hidden from any door cameras or CCTV or conceal his true stature."

"He's deliberately wearing dark clothing, too." DC Rowland Hill, a young officer who had recently transferred from the Derbyshire force to North Yorkshire Serious Crime, announced. "There's no shine to the shoes."

Cyril took another look. "What's the significance of that?"

"He may be wearing shoe coverings to hide evidence."

Cyril nodded.

Owen looked at his own shoes. "He doesn't own any polish. More than fifty percent of the male population never clean their shoes and in the wet and snowy weather we've been having they soon lose their shine."

Hill added some enlarged, still images taken from the footage to the board.

Owen and Cyril moved through to the other Incident Room.

"The more I get to know Dr Green the more I'm convinced these victims may well be linked to the Yorkshire Ripper."

"There was always a belief that what was discovered and what he was convicted for were the tip of the iceberg, Owen. People like that need to increase the score and the closer they sail to the wind the better. Remember the number of times he was questioned, even on one occasion, with his boot in the face of a copper. They even knew the type of boots he wore. That must have given him a feeling of infallibility, as if he were being encouraged on his crusade. It would be lazy and foolish on our part to look to that. Evidence, firm indisputable evidence is all I'll accept.

I'm not hanging this on a convenient hook, whether Dr Green thinks so or not. Technology within forensics is on our side and it's growing more accurate, more capable of searching into the past and finding the truth. We must use every opportunity and facility at our disposal." Cyril turned. "The truth will out, Owen. The truth will out, especially on my watch."

**

Mary Bailey's flight had been delayed leaving France. As the aircraft banked approaching Leeds Bradford Airport it shuddered, owing to the severe turbulence on breaching the grey, layer of cloud. For the first time, in what seemed an age, she could see land through the rain-streaked window. She experienced a flush of relief yet still felt the need to search for the sick bag in the pocket in front of her. She felt hot, sweaty and she seemed to be constantly yawning as if in an attempt to find some fresh and cool air with which to fill her lungs. There was another sudden drop and the wing lifted. The immediate sound of mechanical movement somewhere beneath her made her instinctively lift her feet. At the best of times she tolerated air travel, but on days like this she hated every second. The features on the ground grew in scale and seemed to move with greater speed, first the fields, a patchwork quilt and then the houses and roads. Her stomach churned and she prayed for the wheels to touch down. For the third time she whispered, "Never again" but she knew it to be a lie. The drive from her home in France to Harrogate was even worse. She had left that to her husband.

On leaving the airport she sucked in lungfuls of fresh air before looking across the open expanse before her. It was as if she had never been away. Yorkshire seemed to have an identity all of its own. Granted, the roads had gained far more potholes than she remembered but the route down to Pool-in-Wharfdale and then to Harrogate seemed reassuringly familiar on each of her visits.

Turning the hire car into the drive brought a true realisation as to why she had travelled so far on such a terrible day. The house, in all its grandeur, filled the windscreen, but she was aware that on this occasion, there would be no Auntie Betty ebulliently welcoming her in, insisting she sit by the fire all before killing her with utter kindness. The thoughts brought a tear and she stayed still trying to come to terms with the reality of the moment. Opening her bag, she found the padded envelope in which was the key to the front door and the detailed instructions from Betty Cole's solicitor. She had read them many times.

Chapter 15

April had quickly called an informal meeting to clarify some finer details.

"Patricia Melling was born in Bradford in 1953. We know she attended Wellington Road Primary School and then Bolling Girls' School. She applied and was successful in attending Ripon C of E Teacher Training College starting in September, 1971. She was eighteen. From what we can discover from records and from past students – they have an active social media page – she was placed in halls of residence but was reclusive and shy. Few people could convey any real picture of her true character, she was the same in school. She stayed until the Easter of 1972. After that date she did not return." April flicked through the notes. "We know the reason for that as it was filed and I quote – *'Patricia Melling notified the college of her desire to cease attending the course – At the request of the student. (Personal reasons but no further details given. May, 1972).'* This is likely to be college terminology as it did have a quota set within the annual entry for, shall we say, dropouts, those realising they were not cut out for the teaching profession and those considered to be unsuitable."

Brian Smirthwaite leaned forward and pushed the notes to one side. "So, if we believe she was pregnant at that point when she failed to return, as we know the child was born late 1972, why were the letters we found in the airing cupboard always dated March? Why would she write letters she knew she'd never send to her child, a child she really didn't know even on its first birthday and why add that date? It doesn't match up."

"Date of conception, possibly? It also means the father could have been any student attending at that time."

April watched as Brian counted the months on his fingers. "Brian?"

"The letters in the shoe box were also dated December and that would make a great deal more sense. There's no hint of the father's identity, it's as if it's been completely wiped from history, as if it's an irrelevance. Could it have been rape?"

There was a pause as the possibility was considered.

Shakti interjected. "We know she married Philip Spencer in May, 1974. Where they met and how she came to be in Harrogate, we've yet to establish. We do know she did some voluntary work in a local school and in the central library after that date and I believe her mother-in-law found her work at ICI here in the town. However, we do not have a record for any formal paid employment. I've requested a deeper search looking at National Insurance and HRNC."

"Now that we have a rough timeline for her, how does it compare with that of Philip Spencer?" Cyril's question conveyed little conviction.

"He was born in 1949 in Shipley but they moved to Harrogate when he was young and went through a number of schools in the Harrogate area. His parents separated when he was quite young and he remained with his mother. She worked for ICI Fibres, then a huge company within the town and based where Hornbeam is now. Crimple House was part of the company. She worked there until the early eighties. ICI in Harrogate were licensed producers of Bri-Nylon and Terylene as well as Crimplene, the name derived probably from Crimple House and the area connection I'm assuming."

Cyril tapped his pen on the table. "Fascinating as this might be, April, can we move on to the more pertinent."

There was a sudden silence apart from the constant hum from those working within the room.

"I believe it will become relevant, sir." She looked at Cyril and then Shakti. "Spencer seemed always to work within fabric or clothing manufacture, initially with the firm Robert Hirst. The company was taken over in 1977. I expect that was a worrying time for a young couple only married for three years with a mortgage to pay but he was fortunate and continued to be employed by the new company in his original role as travelling sales representative. He stayed within the firm until 2014 when he retired." She could see Cyril growing more restless but he had requested the time lines for the couple and he was going to hear what she had discovered. "What we do know is that as a child, Philip was taken to Saltaire Hospital after having an allergic reaction to a tetanus injection. We're assuming it was horse serum owing to the date." She paused letting the information percolate and she saw Cyril immediately sit up.

"The disc found at the site – *on no account must this*

person have horse serum. Do you have a date for that?" Cyril was now eager to hear more.

"1955. They moved to Harrogate not long afterwards."

For the first time since the beginning of the meeting, Cyril smiled.

***

Even in the dark, Rodney Crookson paused at the top of Cole's driveway. A shiver momentarily ran down his back as he saw the lounge curtains drawn closed. Seeing them sparked the memory of finding her body; that moment of discovery still lingered in his mind. The parked car reminded him that Betty's niece had arrived from France, a detail he had forgotten before that moment. He wondered what would become of the home, the house next door. He had a dreadful feeling it would be bought and converted into apartments. Suddenly, he felt the morning cold build with the anger the thought brought with it as he tugged at the lead dragging the dog away from the gatepost.

Mary Bailey had slept better than she could have hoped. She had been anxious about returning to such a large house, a house that had witnessed a murder. To her surprise, there had been a familiarity to the bedroom, it was possibly the aroma, a smell she always associated with the happy times she had spent there. It brought with it the sense of security and comfort even though the house had been the scene of her aunt's killing. In all the years she had visited, the house had never really changed. There had been the odd new coat of paint or alteration of certain fabrics but the furnishings had been those of Betty's parents. She thought immediately of her grandfather as she glanced around at the paintings, the mahogany furniture and the clocks. They all seemed to hold his DNA. The thought of Sir Henry, 'Biggles', she had called him as a child, much to his amusement, brought a smile. She embraced a photograph from the sideboard. It was black and white, of Biggles dressed in his air force finery. It was hard to believe he and Betty had once been young. She brought the photograph to her lips and kissed the glass.

"Miss you. How sad you'd be to hear of your dear daughter's death." She clutched the photograph to her for a few moments longer.

Today would involve meetings, here at the house. The police wanted a chat, they had said. It would also be a day of sorting Betty's personal and intimate belongings and waiting for Andrew, her husband, to arrive with the car and the dog.

There was a knock at the front door. She adjusted her dressing gown, checked her hair in a mirror and went down the hall.

"Mary, how lovely to see you. I know it's early. I hope I'm not disturbing you. Our condolences. Goodness it was so tragic." Jennifer Crookson stood in the doorway holding a Tupperware box.

"Come in out of the cold. And to see you. How are you, Mrs Crookson?"

"Jennifer, please. It's not been easy I must admit. I've brought you some scones and I just wanted to say … well. Rodney saw your car earlier this morning when he walked the dog and, well … If there's anything we can do … yes, you know where we are. Is Andrew coming over?"

Mary smiled taking the box. "Thank you for these, that's kind of you. Even though he has only recently returned home from the UK, he is and should be here soon, he's bringing the car and the dog. He rang to say he was an hour away. How is Mr Crookson? It must have been such a shock for him finding Auntie. They've known each other for such a long time."

"Since he had the shops and even before then. He's remarkably resilient. I suppose it comes with running his own business all those years and dealing with the public. I'm sure the discovery had an effect on him but I know he will never let it show. Thank you for asking. Remember, if you need shopping, we're only next door." She smiled.

Closing the door, Mary paused. The thought of Rodney finding the body made her shudder, the reality suddenly overpowering her as she stood in the empty hallway. She broke down in tears. The memories of Rodney too brought with it another shiver, but also a bitter taste in her mouth, the same acrid taste whenever she thought of him.

***

For Cyril, the realisation that they now had a leading clue brought not only jubilation but also a degree of confusion. It seemed fine knowing there was a possibility the silver disc could have belonged to Spencer, therefore tentatively tying him to the Kex Gill crime scene. It was now a case of proving it. Then again, proving he had carried out or was in some way involved in the killings was another even more daunting task. The contradiction of character traits did not worry Cyril. He had known many Jekyll and Hyde types during his police career. He had met people who had lived two lives, they had two wives, two homes in different parts of the country so the possibility of someone committing murder in the morning and returning home as a loving husband in the evening was very plausible.

"So, can we now scratch out Sutcliffe as a possible suspect?" Owen stood with his arms folded. In some ways he had secretly hoped they had discovered more of the Yorkshire Ripper's early crimes.

"It's my belief, considering the evidence we have, we're looking for someone else."

Owen frowned, still not convinced they could disregard him as the possible killer.

"It's only belief, you can pursue what you think. It's based on the evidence we have and as far as I'm concerned, it's a copycat. None of the victims would have worn the disc that was dug up at the site. According to the medical information on them we hold, none was allergic. Spencer was and he certainly had the opportunity to be there but the question we must answer is, did he have the inclination and if he did, what reason would draw a hardworking, charitable man to commit such heinous crimes on people not much younger than himself?"

"Sex. You made an assumption because of all the character reports, that his relationship with his wife was loving. We have no evidence of that, sir."

Cyril nodded. "And you know what thought did? It followed a muck cart thinking it was a wedding but you're right, Owen."

Owen smiled. "My Nan used to say that. There's another thing concerning one of the team, the new face, DC

Hill. He was considering the details of the wording on Spencer's hand and the list Shakti suggested. He's into crosswords and all that and he said if it is the word Bleak before House then it could connect with what he termed a kid's home on a road in Richmond ... Sepulchre Crescent. To some locals, it was known as Bleak Row."

"Sepulchre, a tomb. Where you would lay the dead. Bleak, yes." Cyril leaned back. He turned to April with a new found smile. "We may have progress."

"Sorry to disappoint, sir, but it no longer exists as a supermarket was built on the land where it stood a few years back but we do have another lead."

***

Mary checked her phone and read the text message from Andrew again. One hour. *If he's lucky,* she thought as she made a coffee. She then heard the sound of a car crunching down the gravel driveway.

"Speak of the devil," she whispered, removing the coffee mug from her lips and making a rush for the front door. Andrew waved from the driver's seat. The dog, a cockerpoo, could be heard but not seen. She opened the driver's door.

"That's a bloody long way but at least there's less traffic through the night. If I were to be honest, I enjoyed it. Are you okay?" He climbed out, stretched and kissed her on the forehead. "First things first, old Grumpy in the boot could do with a wee."

The dog needed no encouragement to leave the cage placed in the car boot and found the nearest bush before turning to greet Mary.

"I have missed you, Teak."

Andrew emptied the cases from the boot and popped them in the hall. "I smell coffee and I could kill some toast."

"Would a freshly baked buttered scone do?" Mary asked as she headed for the kitchen closely followed by Teak who paused momentarily by the lounge door, barked and quickly ran into the kitchen.

"You made them?" He sounded surprised as he had not detected the smell of baking when he had entered.

"No, a gift from the neighbours, Jennifer and Dodgy Rodney."

"You've never liked him, have you?" Andrew leaned on the door frame looking into the lounge before entering and opening the curtains. He focused his attention on the carpet looking for evidence of the murder. There was a clear fade line close to the window where the edge of a rug had once been placed.

"No, I never have and if you're looking for clues, Sherlock, I'm afraid you'll be disappointed, they took away the rug, the crime scene people. I'm glad too. I think we should have coffee in the kitchen for now. What's strange is I still can't believe she's gone. People like that shouldn't die, they should fade away slowly but to be murdered ..." She wrapped her arms around herself as if seeking solace. Andrew moved across the room and led her back into the kitchen.

Chapter 16

David Owen walked towards his desk, pausing when he saw the antique style wooden boxes positioned neatly next to a piece of paper placed there by DC Henry Jones.

Found these in a charity shop in York. Took me by surprise!
Chat later.
Henry

Owen picked up the first box. 'Vintage Alphabet Set'. The box looked old but somehow it felt new. There were no knocks, chips or scuffs that would naturally be manifested over a period of time if owned by a child. In places the wood had lost its colour as if faded with age. However, on turning the box over, he read, 'Made in China'. He chuckled. "Sherlock Bloody Holmes, Owen". Opening it he saw a number of wooden sticks, cuboid in shape. On one end of each was a letter or punctuation mark, on the other was the matching rubber-embossed letter. Looking at the ink staining he could see they had been used. He counted the pieces of wood, there were seventy, twenty-six lower case, the same upper case and then a selection of punctuation marks.

"Deliver to the promised land," he announced and a number of colleagues sitting nearby turned. "Did anyone see Henry deliver these?" He held up both boxes.

The closest officer spoke first. "Said he'd be back by ten. He suggested you google 'vintage alphabet set'."

"Thanks." Owen was just about to log on when DC Henry Jones entered.

"You've found them. I've just got back from a few days' leave and I saw them in a charity shop. Couldn't believe my eyes as it brought April's case immediately to mind. I think if this type of stamps were used, the perpetrator would need at least three sets; the blocks could then be taped together to form one stamp or five separate words. It just seems so clumsy." He looked at Owen and then at the stamps. "We need an ink pad."

Owen looked surprised as Henry pulled one from his pocket. "That's what I've been looking for." He dropped it on the desk, a huge self-congratulatory smile on his face.

"You've made my morning, Henry. I think you should let April know."

"She's out. She's interviewing Betty Cole's niece, Mary Bailey. who arrived yesterday from France, that's why I left them with you, sir. What amazed me is the fact you can buy a set for less than a tenner." He pointed to the boxes. "Just pure chance I saw them in the shop window."

Owen made up the word 'promised' and held them together before dipping them onto the ink pad. "Give me your hand, Henry." Carefully, he allowed the stamps to sit on the skin with a gentle pressure. They both inspected the results.

"Bloody hell! I need to check the pictures showing the printing on the victims' forehead. From what I remember, it looks fairly similar to me."

Henry simply brought his hand closer to his face. "I hope this comes off before the wife sees it!"

***

April turned on the driveway and parked behind the French registered estate car. She heard the yap of a dog as she moved towards the front door. Before she had the chance to knock, the door opened. Andrew Bailey smiled immediately. "Inspector Richmond?" He turned his head slightly as if waiting to be challenged.

"Yes, I have an appointment with Mary."

"I saw you arrive. Mary mentioned you were coming. We're methodically working our way through her Aunt's more personal possessions. It's amazing how much can be acquired in a lifetime. Do come in. I'll let her know you're here. May I offer you a tea or coffee? We're having one. A cold morning. Crisp, I believe they're called."

"Indeed. thank you, yes. Coffee, black, no sugar would be perfect."

April settled in the lounge; it was warm and peaceful. The room appeared to be trapped in a time warp with its mixture of historical fashions, a blend that oozed conservative wealth; the paintings, the furnishings even down to the personal items, all appeared to have been collected over many years and from different parts of the world. Despite this, they brought a pleasing ambience. April focused on a small stool before her. She could not fail to see the carved wooden mouse, it appeared to be scampering up one of the legs. On the table by the window were some playing cards set out as if clock patience were being played. She studied them to see where she would make the next move until she heard a dog bark, appearing at the door but seeming reluctant to enter the room. April moved from the table encouraging the dog to enter but it waited at the threshold, its tail between its legs.

"What's the matter, Teak? Nobody will bite you!" Mary spoke encouragingly but the dog turned and disappeared into the hallway. "Detective Inspector, sorry to keep you waiting and sorry for Teak's rudeness. Since we arrived, he's refused to enter this room." Mary placed the tray onto a coffee table.

"They have a sixth sense. My dog's owner was murdered. The dog refuses to walk past the building even now."

April saw her look of consternation. "Murdered?"

"It's a long story." April cupped her coffee mug. "Thank you."

"How may I help?" Mary sat opposite.

The conversation predominantly featured Betty Cole, her life and her interests. April had compiled a list of names and words she had included in the interview in the hope they might work as an aide-mémoire. It was on mentioning Bleak House she noticed an immediate response. Mary sat up and leaned forward as if a light had been shone on a distant memory.

"Bleak House. Goodness, yes. I'd forgotten about that. I once visited but it wasn't called that then, it was just referred to as that by Auntie and some others, but I discovered that only later. It was on Sepulchre Road or was it, Crescent? Anyway, it was a mother and baby home, young children, the unwanted, pregnant young girls. I went in the school holidays with Auntie Betty but of course I didn't understand the significance then. Children were born there to be fostered or adopted. Auntie was like one of the Charity's Governors, or was it termed guardian? I don't recall accurately. I think her job was to check the administration and to ensure everything was done properly. Granddad came that day too, he drove. He always made me travel sick as he thought he was still flying." She chuckled at the thought. "It was actually called Gules House but the name was removed from the gates for some reason, probably to maintain anonymity. These things come to mind later in life when you reflect on your past. The name had something to do with the Richmond coat of arms; to do with the colour red, but you could easily see why people would misinterpret that."

The name 'Red House' immediately came to April wondering if to some it was given that sobriquet.

"The locals knew the road on which the Victorian house stood as Bleak Row, but I believe that went back well before the house was built. I never really knew why, it closed down not long afterwards but I couldn't be sure as to the actual date."

April produced photographs of the two other victims, giving no information about their identity. All had been found at their addresses and some were taken when they were younger. Mary picked up each in turn.

"I know this person. Give me a minute. Murphy, Meridale … something like that. He worked at the home but much later, when it was closing and prior to demolition. He also came here, to Auntie's."

"Meredith?" April decided a prompt was appropriate, her guesses were close enough.

"Yes, that's it. Now I remember. It's Stan. Later, when I met him here, he had moved to Harrogate."

"In what capacity?" April leaned forward. She was making progress.

"I don't know. I remember he used to arrive on a motorcycle and sidecar."

"May I ask how old you are?" April needed confirmation.

"Fifty-six. Born in 1968. Mum was younger than Auntie."

"You don't know the other gentleman?"

Mary shook her head. "Sorry. My aunt was very active in many areas, she had the financial means. She never really worked for a living, she used to give of her time freely, hence the MBE. Being a spinster, she also got the family home."

April detected a degree of resentment, bitterness possibly handed down from mother to daughter.

"Are you aware Rodney Crookson found your aunt's body?"

Immediately April detected a sudden tension in Mary's posture and a swift change in her facial expression.

"Have you seen him, and if you have, did he mention anything about the discovery?"

Mary sat back in the chair. There was a pause that seemed to stretch for too long.

***

Owen placed one of the boxes before Cyril.

"You can see from the photograph of Betty Cole's forehead and Henry's hand where he tested the stamp, they're a close match. Made in China, practically for nothing, a fiver, I believe when I checked them out on the web. I've sent one box to Forensics to see if they can be more precise."

Cyril inspected the box. "A lucky find. The question is why? Why go to the trouble of stamping the way they did when it leaves a greater chance of being discovered?"

"Whoever killed them wants to be caught. Paying back in some way? Righting wrongs?"

"If they were righting wrongs, Owen, they'd be sending them in the opposite direction from the promised land. The victims all seemed to be good people."

"Unless they're sending them to a certain place, a place they had promised … 'one day I'll send you to hell in a handcart'." Owen folded his arms.

"That's another historical reference, Owen. It's linked to the plague. What with Dickens' 'Bleak House' and this." Lifting one of the wooden letters, he then picked up the photograph of the word printed on Henry Jones's hand. "Have you requested a comparison of the ink on Spencer's hand with the impressions made by these blocks?"

"The ink on Spencer's hand was from his favourite pen which we found in the charity shop. If you recall it was mentioned in the forensic report." For the first time, Owen saw Cyril's face flush.

"I should read with greater care, Owen."

"The ink used here is from a pad Henry found. There'll be no link to the case."

***

April collected the photographs but left them in a group on the table. "Have I touched a nerve, Mary."

There was another pause and Mary put her hands to her head.

"Look, it's nothing but I can't see or speak with Crookson without experiencing a sudden feeling of nausea. When I was younger." She stopped.

April, sensing she might just clam up, changed tack. "Tell me what you know about him."

"He's been a neighbour since I was born. He and his wife would often have dinner here, especially when grandfather was alive. He had three shops, maybe more. Worked with a business partner. The company had been started by his father and Rodney went into the family business as a young man. Outfitters, both for ladies and gents. 'Crookson and Cleverly' were well known in the cities of Leeds and Bradford. There was also a branch in Harrogate but that came a little later. According to my mother they used to be very traditional but Rodney saw the possibilities when the sixties and seventies experienced major fashion changes. The swinging sixties. The shops became boutiques and were renamed, 'CC Fashions' and they were very successful."

"Did your mum and dad live in Skipton when they married?"

"Yes, dad worked for the Skipton Building Society. Their head office has always been in the town. I'd spend some of my summer holidays here with Auntie, she was such great fun and when I was old enough, I did some work here. She managed to get me a Saturday job at CC Fashions in town."

April sensed her mood suddenly change. "You were how old?" She now knew the direction the conversation was about to take.

"Sixteen. Sweet sixteen. Auntie would often take me home after work or on the Sunday but there was one occasion when she couldn't. Mum was busy and dad was poorly, he'd been diagnosed with multiple sclerosis. He had good and bad times but Mr Crookson offered to drive me."

April did a quick mental calculation assuming Crookson to be about eighty. He would have been forty when Mary was sixteen.

"I was excited as he had a flash car, a red Ferrari Dino, it sounded supersonic to me. I suddenly felt grown up and exhilarated by it all but on the way home he—" She paused. "I'm sorry, you wanted to talk about Auntie not the silly escapades of a teenager."

April said nothing for a few moments. "What you're telling me and what I'm understanding could be of significance. Did he try to molest you?"

"I had started to feel sick. As I said, he had a flash car and he drove faster than grandfather ever did. I told him that I felt sick. 'I know where we can stop if you can hang on a bit,' he said and he slowed down. Just after Swinsty, the reservoir at Blubberhouses, he pulled into a layby and I went into an area of woods to the side of the road. I felt foolish. One minute I was in a beautiful car and feeling grown up and special and then … He had followed me and started to rub my back but then his hands moved gently round and found my breasts. I was shocked. Initially I couldn't move I remember. His hand then moved down to between my legs. I turned round and vomited all over him. Since that day, I can't see or meet him without feeling sick."

"Does he ever say anything about this now?"

"To him, it's always been as if it never happened and if he does think of it I'm sure he would consider it normal and acceptable."

"Did you mention it to your mother or Auntie?"

"No, I thought I would get into trouble, as if it were my fault or for spoiling his clothes as I knew he was so cross. I only worked a couple more Saturdays but that was enough. I made an excuse and mum allowed me to find a job in Skipton."

"So, nobody knew?"

Mary shook her head. She collected the photographs from the table and selected that of Stanley Meredith. "Stanley was always very kind. I asked him once for a ride in his sidecar but he refused. He told me young ladies should travel in style and not in his contraption. He was always so sweet. Please don't mention what I have said to Mr Crookson, well not until everything is sorted. Time has moved on and I wouldn't agree to take it further … what happened in the past taught me a lesson and—"

April did not reply but collected the photographs and stood. "Thank you. Will you be staying here long?"

"We have to check my aunt's possessions and then secure the house. These things can take inordinate amounts of time but I believe her estate was in order and she did make a will. We still have an apartment in Skipton, Andrew uses it when he's over on business."

"What will happen to this beautiful house?" April turned and looked around the room.

"Other people's possessions can be a burden, especially the private papers and personal memories. I'll have to break the bond of sentimentality, I feel. We love living in France and England is different now and continues to change so much I feel and not for the better. If Andrew and I were honest, it's not home anymore and with Auntie and mum gone there's nothing to keep us here. It will all be sold apart from a few special personal items."

Teak stood and wagged his tail as April moved towards the front door.

"May I call again, possibly tomorrow morning? There's still one photograph I would like to show you so it would only be a brief visit."

"Certainly." Mary smiled but the gesture conveyed little enthusiasm.

As the front door closed, Andrew appeared at the top of the stairs. "Is everything alright? She was here a long time."

"Not a problem. It seems as though they've no idea who killed Betty or the other two. Did you ever meet Stanley Meredith?"

"I think I did come to think of it. Didn't he fight in the Falklands and ride a motorcycle and sidecar?" He moved into the lounge and stood in front of the cards on the table. He moved some. Within minutes all the cards fell into place. He turned to Mary. "It came out! Fate is simply wonderful, that mixed with a degree of luck of course. You have to have some luck in life."

She moved across and kissed him. "Well done, you. We've work to do."

Chapter 17

"Well, well, well, Randy Rodney," Shakti announced on hearing the story. "Hell's bells, if I had a pound for every time I was hit on when I was a student by some elderly bloke whilst working in a restaurant in the holidays, I wouldn't need to be here. Seems a strange coincidence he stopped at the same location as the discovered remains." She dunked a piece of bread into a cup full of soup. "Breakfast and dinner in one!"

"It's the only stopping place until you get to the top of Kex Gill and if someone's going to throw up in your flash new car you stop as soon as and wherever you can. Sorry, you're eating. I had to google 'Ferrari Dino' – goodness what a car."

Shakti nodded. "Takes forever for the smell to go, irrespective of how posh it is. I've travelled in police cars that ponged for ages of puke kindly donated by drunks on a Saturday night. They say pouring a can of coke over the area gets rid of the aroma but I'd rather not have to try."

"I've heard that as well. Mary knew Meredith, too. Nothing but good to say about him. I need to show her the photograph of Patricia Spencer. I just have this feeling, more of a long shot. Crookson had a shop in Bradford when she lived there." She glanced at Shakti. "I know, I know, the chances are slim but I have to try."

"At least you'll have an answer one way or another. We've had no luck chasing down any formal work she might have done. Checked the tax and she's not in a pension scheme, we've found nothing other than what we know already." Shakti put down the mug and moved to the desk removing some photographs. "This should be of interest. We found these when going through boxes of photographs stashed in Spencer's loft. They were in 35mm slide format but they've been digitally enhanced and printed by the techies. They're fresh off the press, so to speak. It looks like a trade fashion or clothing exhibition. We know it's at the exhibition centre here in the town from what we can identify. The colours are still strong and they're relatively sharp."

April looked at each one. "Is that … I wonder who the group of ladies is? Look at the fashion, late 60's maybe early 70's would you say?"

"We believe so. It's a young Patricia Melling. It's the hair styles and look at the mannequins in the cabinets, all flairs and lapels. How times change. If she wasn't working, what was she doing there at a trade show? She looks so young. There are some other slides but they've suffered a degree of damage, possibly water ingress. We're trying to resurrect them. We'll have to wait for those."

April began attaching them to the whiteboard, drawing a line to the name 'Patricia Spencer (Melling)'.

"And Andrew, what does he do?" Shakti asked, finally draining her soup.

"Wine merchant. They have a rather nice chateau, I

believe, and also a flat in Skipton. He imports, a bit like a salesman but he works for himself. A middleman better sums him up. He stays in the flat when he's working in the north. I don't think they're short of a bob or two and I know they won't be once the sale of Betty Cole's estate goes through."

***

Cyril parked his car some distance down Duchy Road from the Crooksons' property. The early afternoon sky was the uniform colour of lead but that overcast had brought a marginal rise in the temperature though it was still cold. The black and white mock Tudor frame of the Ladies' College seemed to dominate the area to the left. Further up on the right was his destination, set behind a mature hedge of evergreen. He had liaised with Brian Smirthwaite who felt his own attendance might only aggravate the situation; Cyril had already met Crookson and knew just what to expect.

Crookson was standing at the front bay window looking out onto the garden and the drive as Cyril paused and viewed him from the other side of the hedge. He seemed to be admiring the evergreens within the herbaceous border, the only islands of colour, apart from a robin that stood in the centre of the lawn. Cyril observed his sudden head movement as he entered via the small side gate and noticed he instinctively took a step back into the darker part of the room.

Moments later the front door opened. "Detective Inspector what can we do for you this time?"

Cyril removed his glove before holding out his hand as if

it were a peace offering. Rodney Crookson leaned forward and shook it.

"Detective Chief Inspector. Like with American Indians, the title 'chief' is quite important," Cyril corrected without a hint of cynicism.

"Yes, indeed, chief. My apologies. The memory is not what it was. Do come in out of the cold. Will we get rain or snow today?" There was an insecurity and nervousness in his tone. Cyril did not answer.

"Who is it, Rodney?" his wife called from down the hall.

"It's the police again, dear. We'll be invited to their staff dances the way we're going on. We'll be in the lounge."

Cyril let the comment drift over his head. "I need some information from your past, today." Cyril slipped a Dictaphone from his pocket and placed it on the table between them. "It saves my taking notes and stops any ambiguity later. Do you mind?"

"I'll receive a transcript, I assume?"

Cyril nodded before placing a photograph of Philip Spencer on the table. He tapped it with his finger but said nothing. Rodney slipped on his glasses momentarily and then removed them.

"You've seen this photograph before when my colleague called. Then you told him you had no idea who the man was. Are you sure? Please take a closer look. I believe you were the owner of a number of gents' and ladies' outfitters; boutiques, I believed you renamed them against your father's better judgement but he was wrong on that occasion and your business acumen was sound."

Rodney Crookson looked surprised as he was expecting the interview to be focused on Betty Cole. "Yes, as you say, he was wrong. It was the best move we, as a business, made. We developed the enterprise more than we could have hoped so your information is correct but I fail to see the relevance considering the circumstances. What has that got to do with Betty?"

"It's to do with the man in the photograph."

Crookson picked it up. There was an inordinate pause. "It could be a man by the name of Spencer." He peered over his glasses at Cyril.

"I'm assuming that you know Spencer was murdered in the same manner as Betty Cole."

There was a nod of the head. "I didn't connect the two until you've just—"

"Tell me what you know about him," Cyril interrupted, knowing he needed to keep a firm grip on the interview.

"Spencer was a sales rep for Hirst's, the coat manufacturer here in Harrogate. Before that I knew his mother. She worked for ICI Fibres, she was acquainted with my father, you see. Anyway, Spencer would often come into the shops with samples. The new, modern fabrics were all the rage. We sold children's clothing and the overcoats were marvellous, what with the removable liner and secret pocket." He dropped the photograph back onto the table. "We had a professional relationship, as I had with many reps. But why was he murdered? What would make someone do that?"

Cyril did not answer but posed a question he had been wanting to ask since his arrival. "We believe you employed young women in your shops, Saturday and holiday girls all on a temporary basis."

Rodney frowned, wondering at the sudden change of

direction. He flushed slightly and felt a trickle of sweat run down his inner arm. "We did. In all the shops. When High Streets had shops, that is. You would often find the girls supporting the staff with the more menial tasks, but as you say, not only on Saturdays but during the school holidays. College and University students were valuable to the business."

Cyril removed another photograph showing a group of women at an exhibition. "I believe you were an exhibitor at many of the clothes and fashion shows here in town. Do you recognise anyone in this group?"

A smile came to Rodney's lips. "Goodness, where on earth did … that's a few of the women who worked in my shops. This must have been taken in about 1970 at a guess. You forget how fashions develop and at that time they changed almost monthly. It was wonderful for business. The youngsters seeing their pop idols' fashions, wanted to copy them, be them. In the old days clothes lasted years, but in the sixties and seventies, they had to have the latest fashions. The quality was dreadful but you gave them what they wanted. That's good business."

Cyril sat back. It was as if the image had taken Rodney back. "You were a man in his prime in 1970, a young man responsible for the employment of quite a few young and pretty girls and women. I've heard quite some things about those times, Mr Crookson. The swinging sixties."

Crookson's face immediately changed. "Just what are you insinuating, Detective Chief Inspector?" There was an exaggerated force to the word 'Chief'.

"Were you present when that photograph was taken?"

"Yes, I recall it well on seeing this. I believe Spencer

must have taken it, hence your early question. It was a reward trip for the shop staff. I hired a mini bus. They had afternoon tea at Betty's and toured the exhibition. Having young eyes and ideas helped stock the business, we purchased items based on what they liked. If the Saturday girl or boy wanted to buy our clothing, we knew others would too. I'm a Yorkshireman, I wanted to be successful and I lifted the old shops into a new and very profitable era. Make hay whilst the sun shines, is my motto."

"And did you, Mr Crookson?"

"Did I what?"

"Make hay?" Cyril maintained full eye contact. There was a pause as Rodney shuffled uncomfortably in his chair.

"We had four shops, successful shops and they brought me what you see around you today, so I suppose I did, yes, or were you insinuating something darker. Were you going into the gutter?"

The ringing of Cyril's phone interrupted the moment like the bell ending a round in a boxing match. He answered it quickly, immediately annoyed at the intrusion. "I need to take this." He leaned forward to switch off the Dictaphone keeping his eyes on Crookson's. "Interview temporarily halted," he announced before his finger hit the switch.

"Take what time you need." Rodney stood and exited the room, closing the door as he left.

Cyril sat back and continued with the call.

"We have a DNA link in all the murder sites but what's strange, sir, it's very strong and layered in Dragon Parade. There's past and present, as if whoever did the killings paid more than one visit to that house," Shakti informed him, a degree of excitement in her voice.

"Is there nothing similar in Cole's or Meredith's, only Spencer's?"

"No, just Spencer's."

"The arguments that were reported by the neighbour. Have they found the DNA traces in the areas from which the noise was reported to have come?"

"Investigating further as we speak. There's something else. They've managed to save some of the damaged slides. I'm going to send through some of the more significant ones for you on WhatsApp. You might like to discuss them with Crookson." Shakti hung up.

Moments later the images arrived. There were three. They were clearly taken at the exhibition in question as the girls were dressed in the same clothing but now, they showed a young man with some of the girls. It was clear who the man was. Cyril stood and went to the door. "Thank you. I'll not keep you much longer."

Both Jennifer and Rodney appeared in the hall, neither looked welcoming. Cyril smiled and went back into the lounge. He knew showing the next photographs would elicit a degree of hostility.

***

Owen stood next to Dr Green and yet again admired the colour combination of his clothing. It could be classed as a riot but it seemed to suit him. He slipped on a white lab coat before handing one to Owen.

"The sleeves might be a little short like last time but our clients here are well past caring. I believe you have an ID of the latest body on receiving the DNA. Another female, age confirmed to be twenty. I believe I mentioned we don't have as many remains as the others but we have the skull minus the lower jaw. Belinda, we called her, keeping faith with the original theme. However, I believe she's actually Diane?"

Owen nodded and produced the photograph of the girl at the time she had disappeared. "Diane Sharp. Brought up in Knaresborough. A strange case as she'd been missing on a few occasions before, once for a month when she was fifteen, before that absence was reported to the police. According to her brother, it was something she did on a regular basis but she'd normally come home after a week or so. Followed the popular bands. I think the term is 'groupie'. Strangely, he had a suspicion she'd been murdered by Sutcliffe, the Yorkshire Ripper but the police weren't interested. Prostitutes and ladies of the night they told him not young girls out in the day time."

"How did the police know she was …"

Owen just shrugged his shoulders. "When you look back it seems like the police were responsible for a catalogue of errors. Wouldn't happen under Bennett's watch, that I can tell you for sure."

"We've revised the cause of death. It's still a strike to the head but it's dissimilar to the others, neither a rock in a sock, as your boss puts it, nor the hammer. We believe it to be a cylindrical, metal object similar to this. Most cars during that period carried a spare wheel and all the accoutrements to change it when a puncture occurred. This item is one of those tools."

"A wheel-brace?" Owen said hesitantly.

"Correct. That must be why you're a detective." He winked. "It's the end bit here that suggests something like this was used as the weapon. You can see it's not too dissimilar to a hammer in terms of the shape and the weight. However, Diane was struck more than once."

Green picked up the skull. "If we consider the cranial structure, we have evidence to show the first attempt struck her to the side of the head at about this point, the temporal bone or the squamous. That, Owen, would have knocked her to the ground. The second blow, the coup de grâce, as they say, was a much more focused blow causing severe cranial damage." He held up the skull.

"How do you know the machines, a pick or shovel, didn't cause that?" Owen put his finger into the damaged area.

"Experience suggests it's age related. Had the blow occurred recently, during the excavation, the skull would have fractured. Nothing can be certain but when we use our knowledge of previous cases we can state it's an eighty percent accurate judgement."

Chapter 18

Cyril was already at a table in the corner of The Coach and Horses. It was the first time Owen had been in since the refurbishment. No longer was the metal skeleton riding the penny farthing attached to the outside of the building. He had been saddened to see it removed but, as with all things, changes must come, some not necessarily for the better. It had been altered considerably since their first meetings in the early days, when they did not allow children, games machines or play music. They just served a consistently good pint and fostered the buzz of conversation. The smell of cooking added to the ambience and Owen suddenly felt hungry. He could kill a pie and gravy. Removing his coat, he tossed it over the chairback opposite Cyril.

Cyril nursed a pint of Black Sheep as if someone might steal it at any moment. Looking up he saw his colleague. Owen pointed to his drink, a masculine type of semaphore suggesting he get him another. Cyril moved his finger and thumb a distance apart, signalling just a half was required. No words were spoken.

Owen would normally down one at the bar and then

come to the table with the second but those times had gone since Christopher was born, one was now enough. He tossed two packets of crisps onto the table.

"It's the aroma in here, I could kill a pie but these will have to do. You start first." Owen sipped the head from the beer and wiped his mouth with his jacket sleeve.

"I think, my friend, we've stirred a hornets' nest. I bet Crookson wishes now he hadn't discovered the body in the first place. He eventually admitted to knowing Philip Spencer after a little gentle digging but stressed it was only on a professional level. He blamed the trauma of finding Cole, age and poor memory but then suddenly he could tell us what we knew already."

"And the women?"

"Now here's the thing. They worked for him, some permanent, others were temps; Saturday and holiday casuals. Probably never went through the books. One of those Saturday girls was—"

Owen jumped straight in. "Patricia Melling?"

Cyril chuckled. "She'd be seventeen or eighteen when the exhibition was held, we've tracked the date, it was a year later than Crookson believed. She'd be working in between school and college."

"Did he give her one?" Owen said as he held his pint to the light and admired the colour.

Cyril nearly spit out most of his beer and began to choke as he tried to swallow what remained in his mouth and laugh at the same time. "Diplomacy still top of your skill set, Owen. Strangely enough, you might be surprised to hear he didn't say."

"We know he was a bit of a jack the lad. April mentioned

the assault on Mary Bailey. If she were to report that now, even after all these years, it might be like kicking and burning your hornets' nest. We might be disturbed by what we find." Owen finished his packet of crisps and looked longingly at Cyril's. It did not go unnoticed and Cyril pushed them across the table.

"Starving, thanks. You're now going to ask me if I think he could be linked with the bodies found where he tried it on with Mary." Flecks of masticated crisp shot across the table and landed on Cyril's jacket. "Sorry, bad habit talking with a gob full but you are, I know."

"Well. Do you?"

Owen shook his head whilst two fingers delved into the remnants at the bottom of the packet. "No, he might be a randy bastard but a killer? That always takes something deeper so, no, he had too much to lose. He was married, had a nice home, lovely car and the work couldn't be that taxing. Why spoil all that?" He licked each of his fingers before rubbing them on his coat.

Cyril frowned and then nodded in agreement. Moments later Julie came in. Cyril waved.

"May I join you. It's been a bloody long day." She let her shoulders sag to emphasise the point.

Owen kicked a chair away from the table for her to sit. Julie slipped her coat onto the back and settled down as Owen moved towards the bar returning with a gin and tonic. "It's a double. You look as though you need it." He turned to Cyril. "There's some link between the postage stamps and Spencer's interest in them and his odds and sods collection. What exactly, I'm not sure but the more I think about it the more I'm convinced. You two have a good meal

... Have a pie for me."

***

The hotel room was colder than expected but the view compensated for that inconvenience. Seen yards from the window was the Cenotaph, a dark needle, almost silhouetted against the many lights running down Parliament Street. Remembering the dead seemed at that very moment more than a little apt. Turning away, the wooden box was removed from the small travel case and placed onto the bedside table alongside the semi-opaque packet. Those were the only items needed to complete the night-time task.

Within half an hour, the playing cards were positioned clock-like on the coffee table that had been placed before the window. The clock on Betty's Tearoom showed 8.15. There was plenty of time. Hands began to turn the cards, each action, methodical, deliberate and well-practised.

***

Rodney Crookson walked the dog the final hundred yards down Duchy Road. In one hand he held a small bag, the contents had been scooped from the pavement. They could now return home. Neither he nor the dog wanted to be out. The cold seemed more severe than on previous late-night walks. The figure he could see standing further up the road did not move but leaned against one of the roadside trees. Rodney looked to see if they had a dog for what would they be doing at 11.30 on a cold January night if they were not walking a dog?

Rodney's dog barked once as he tugged the lead, eager to get to the person before pausing momentarily. The figure remained motionless. Before discovering the body and hearing of the other killings, Rodney would not have hesitated on seeing a solitary figure, he would have just walked on but now there was uncertainty and apprehension and, if he were to be honest, fear.

Come on Rodney, you're making a mountain of a molehill. The thought spurred him on. He started walking, stretching to make himself look taller and more positive. Yet the closer he came to the man, the more disturbed he became. He could see the cloud of vapour, the warm breath hitting the cold air, streamed from the person's nostrils. As he approached, he noticed the head turn to face him. The hood on the jacket was up and a scarf wrapped around the mouth.

The dog paused briefly before taking a wide berth around the stationary figure. Rodney also followed suit before offering a tentative, "Good night." There was no response.

When they were at their closest point, a hand suddenly outstretched. Rodney instinctively flinched. There was something in the hand and he became agitated. A hot flush rushed through his body as the dog barked again. Initially, he thought it was a knife but no further movement ensued. Looking at the outstretched hand, Rodney saw it was an envelope.

"Take it!" The instruction was clear and precise. "It's definitely for you."

Holding the lead in one hand and the bag in the other,

Rodney hesitated again.

"You would be wise to do as I ask."

Rodney wanted to run but his legs seemed rooted. His throat was suddenly dry. "I don't know you."

"Drop the bag." He waved the envelope again.

The bag fell to the floor as he took the envelope. Within moments the figure turned and walked down Duchy Road leaving Rodney holding onto an envelope and trying to get his breathing under control. Within minutes he would be home.

"Is that you, Rodney?" Jennifer sounded uncertain.

The dog scampered up the stairs answering her question. She waited listening for the usual signs. She heard none. "Rodney?" She slipped on a dressing gown and tentatively went down stairs. Rodney was sitting on the chair in the hall. He had removed none of his outdoor clothes. He had even left his hat on. She hurried to him, anxiety clear in her movements and voice. "Are you alright, darling?"

Rodney did not move. He looked down at the envelope held in his gloved hands. She knelt by his side. "Rodney?" She removed his hat and placed it on the floor. He did not move. As if in slow motion he turned over the envelope. To the top right corner was an old stamp, it had been franked but the lines failed to travel from the stamp to the envelope, suggesting the stamp was old and reused. The wording was clear. *'They are on their way as I promised.'*

Taking the envelope, she slid her finger and tore the top. She paused. Rodney was now looking directly at the envelope in her hands.

"I was frightened, I thought …"

She carefully removed the contents. Three close-up photographs of the three people killed, Betty Cole, Philip Spencer and Stan Meredith were revealed. The familiar faces seemed to stare at the camera as if frozen in death. Dropping the collection, she brought her hands to her mouth, stifling the involuntary sound that had started deep in her chest. This action brought Rodney to his senses. Wrapping his arms around her he pulled her towards his legs.

"What's going on?" She began to sob.

He gently kissed her on the forehead. "I don't know, I really don't know."

Chapter 19

Cyril was not in bed when the call came through. He had just settled with a glass of brandy, his feet on a low stool as he stared at the Theodore Major painting directly opposite. He focused on the painted moon trapped within the clouds. 'The moon was a ghostly galleon tossed upon cloudy seas …' The words of a poem he had learned as a child came to mind. "Theodore Major could paint," he whispered before sipping his drink. Julie was next to him curled on the sofa; her eyes were closed. It had been a perfect night. As the phone rang, he checked his watch, shook his wrist and looked again. It was 12.20. Julie moved instinctively as he groaned.

"Bennett." There was clearly a reluctance in his tone. He listened whilst at the same time he sat up. He shook Julie. "Just now? Did he give a description? Send a car as soon as." He tossed the phone onto the stool recently vacated by his feet. "Shit!"

"Is there nobody else who could go?" The frustration was clearly evident as Julie stretched and got to her feet.

Cyril was already tying his shoelaces. He looked at her. "Crookson has had a visit. All the signs suggest it was from the killer."

"Is he hurt?" Julie now understood his urgency. She collected his coat and scarf.

"That's just it. The person intercepted him whilst he was walking his dog. Thirty minutes ago, max."

"How does he—"

"It's what he handed to him. If we can get some kind of description and act with speed, we might just be able to find the killer."

Julie saw the blue lights flash outside the window. "Your car's here. They must have phoned you on the way."

Less than five minutes later the car pulled onto Crookson's drive. A marked police car was already in attendance. An officer was standing by the front door. Cyril was pleased with the efficiency; no chances were being taken.

Crookson was sitting in the lounge, in the same seat he had occupied earlier. He held a drink in his hand; it looked like whisky. Jennifer was sitting with another officer. Immediately Cyril saw the envelope on the coffee table and instinctively removed a pair of nitrile gloves from his pocket.

"Frightened me to bloody death, Detective Chief Inspector. Sorry it's you who's been dragged from your bed. In all the time I've walked the dog I've never experienced anything quite like it. The person's lack of movement, the silence. They were neither hostile nor aggressive. If I see anyone out that late, they too are walking a dog. This person was just leaning against the roadside tree. To be honest I had to look twice. The dog barking made me realise it was a person. I could then see the plumes of vapour from their breath." He pointed to his nostrils.

"Male or female?" Cyril had removed his notebook and jotted the time and date.

"They were hooded and they had a scarf round their mouth but I immediately assumed it to be male. Dark clothes, gloves too probably owing to the cold."

"Height and build?"

Shorter than me so maybe 5ft 9 or 10 but I'm not sure. Average build but as I say, he was well wrapped up so you couldn't really tell."

Cyril turned to the officer. "Get a call out with that description. Stop anyone whether alone or not who might be a match. Call Control also. I want an inventory ASAP of people who have booked into hotels and Bed and Breakfast accommodation tonight as a single occupant. Start with the immediate town centre and then work out from there. We have run the check before so the procedure is already in place." The officer stood and smiled at Jennifer before moving out into the hallway.

"He just waited until I was level with him and he handed me that." Rodney pointed to the envelope and then took a sip from his glass.

Cyril picked up the envelope with great care and read what was printed on the front. It was stamped in a similar font to that seen on each victim.

They are on their way as I promised.

"And before you ask, I have no idea what that's supposed to mean and look at the stamp, it's been used in the past. It's not a modern one."

Cyril scrutinised the stamp. He paused immediately. The orange-coloured design was an unusual shape, rectangular rather than square and marked 5d, pre decimal so before 1972. To one corner was the gold silhouette of a young Queen Elizabeth next to the dates, 1812/1870 and the name, Charles Dickens. He had no idea who was depicted on the stamp but his mind went straight to Bleak House. He was not surprised to see the stamp had been franked but there was no evidence of the franking on the envelope.

"What was inside made a little more sense to me or should I say relevance. That printing is not too dissimilar to what was on Betty's forehead. I remember seeing the word 'promised' on Betty, but to be honest, the words had not registered until I saw this envelope. Jennifer thinks I blanked things out through shock … it was that word 'promised' that brought it all back. The stamp too."

Removing the contents, Cyril immediately recognised the faces of the three murder victims. The photographs were obviously taken by the killer at the scene of the crime. The next image seemed in stark contrast. It was of a young woman holding a newborn child. He held it closer in the hope of getting more light on the picture. It was black and white. It was clearly a facsimile made from an older photograph. He had an immediate idea who the woman was. The following photographs, four in number, were very different.

"Why me?" Crookson looked directly across the table.

Cyril could clearly see genuine confusion and fear in his eyes. The liquid in the glass Rodney held was never perfectly level, it seemed to be constantly moving; Rodney's hand still demonstrated a slight tremor. Cyril said nothing but held the photograph of the young woman so Crookson could see it. "I believe you knew this woman many years ago. I believe you employed her."

Rodney frowned but barely focused on the image. "I'm sorry, I've no idea and I'm not in the mood for guessing games. I could have been killed tonight just like the others."

"But you weren't and there's obviously a reason for that and that reason is trapped within the envelope you were given. It's too late now, but tomorrow morning I shall be sending a car for you. I want to question you at the station."

"Station? I've done nothing wrong other than co-operate with you and your colleagues over the last few days."

Cyril slipped the photographs back in the envelope in the order in which they had been removed.

"You're helping us catch a killer, someone who might kill again. Interviews carried out at the station are far better for us, we have greater resources."

Rodney downed the remnants of the glass. "Will I need a solicitor?"

"Unless you're guilty of a crime of which I'm unaware, I don't think that will be necessary but if it would make you more comfortable, you are more than welcome."

Cyril stood, slipped the envelope into a forensic evidence bag and moved to the door. "For your peace of mind, I will instruct an officer to remain here until you are collected in the morning. I'll also arrange for an officer to be with your wife tomorrow whilst you're at the station, again for your peace of mind."

Jennifer stood. "Thank you, I'll be fine and thank you for your help and understanding. I'll appreciate the company tomorrow." She put a smile on her lips but it was forced. "If we could only turn back time, Detective Chief Inspector."

Cyril paused, looked at her and nodded. "Indeed."

***

Cyril woke before the alarm. He had managed to get back home to bed but it felt as though his eyes had only just closed. Julie was already in the kitchen. She appeared with a cup of tea and placed it next to him, before kissing his forehead. "A kiss, the stamp of my sincere love."

Cyril stiffened. "Say that again."

"What? A kiss on the forehead I always feel is so significant, mothers kiss their offspring there, there's something sincere, special. You kiss me there often, probably instinctively."

"But you used the word stamp."

"Yes, love letters, postcards convey love but they need a stamp. We convey our love and that's passed on, shown, stamped through a kiss." She paused. "Cyril, it's early, so forgive my mumbled chatter. Drink your tea, it's gone seven." She went back into the kitchen.

Cyril closed his eyes briefly. He thought of the stamp he had seen on the envelope and the title, Charles Dickens. Was it just another coincidence or had it been selected deliberately? If so, why.

As he left, Cyril kissed Julie on the forehead and winked.

"You'd be amazed how often you do that without thinking about it, Bennett. It's instilled in us all. When you have a minute this morning, google 'mothers kissing their newborn', when you get to work."

Cyril frowned before waving a hand and disappearing into the morning dark.

Chapter 20

As Julie had suggested before he left the house, Cyril stared at the computer screen. She had been right, the majority of images showed the mothers kissing the head or forehead of their newborn, an affirming stamp of affection, a bonding action. He also thought of the times he had kissed Julie in the same way, without a thought but in some ways the act was full of meaning. He closed Google and looked at the photographs he had taken of the envelope and those images received by Crookson, concentrating on the stamp. It had to have been chosen for a reason. The evidence from the crime scenes suggested that what had been executed was planned or controlled, from the way the victims were attacked, the markings and … the stamp; were they signs or symbols; stepping stones or some bizarre cryptic announcement to lead them in a certain direction? The only question was, to what or to where?

Lifting his glasses onto his head, he checked the time before moving through to the open office. Harry Nixon was already working and Brian Smirthwaite had just arrived. He motioned for Brian to come to Harry's desk. After a brief explanation of the occurrences of the previous evening, he turned to them both.

"I need an in-depth search of Spencer's house, the warrant is still in place." He held up his hands as if admitting it might seem a foolish request. "I know it's been searched to within an inch of its life but there's something missing. We've found the letters, the postcards, the collection of stamps and the slides but something is staring us in the face and we just can't see it."

Brian pulled up a chair. "I've been all over it, so too has Shakti. She trawled the slides from a corner of the loft."

"There's something, I just know it." He removed his phone and showed them the pictures he had taken the previous evening of the envelope and images handed to Crookson. "Look at the stamp. It's placed deliberately. The date they were published was 1970, the centenary of Dickens's death. We know it's from the person who killed Cole, Spencer and Meredith. No one else would have been in a position to take images of the dead."

"Some coppers have in the past and posted them—"

Cyril's look was enough to stop the outburst from Brian.

"But it's these photographs that make me feel we need another search." He held out his phone. Both men leaned closer to look at the first image on his phone.

"Melling?"

Cyril nodded. "It is, and we'll have confirmation as soon as they've done a computer scan comparison from the photographs we have of her."

"If that's her child, that would make it around 1972, so why the stamp if it were introduced in 1970?"

"We can assume Melling started work at Crookson's shop around that time," Brian suggested with a degree of uncertainty.

"And what else?" Harry's tone left no doubt what he was suggesting. "Born 1953 so she'd be—"

"Seventeen," Brian interrupted. "Crookson would have been twenty-seven, good looking, wealthy and her boss, a man with influence and a degree of charisma and in a prime position to take advantage of naïve, young women."

"He was also married," Harry added.

Cyril raised his eyebrows. "But he was married when he tried it on with his neighbour's niece so let's not stand him on a pedestal just yet. I've sent April to be with Jennifer, his wife, whilst he's here." He showed them only one other photograph.

"Who's that?" Harry asked, leaning closer to the screen.

"That's a good question, Harry. Another stepping stone to the truth, maybe."

"Really?"

"Really. Have they completed a thorough sweep of Meredith's place yet?"

Both men shook their heads. "In the process."

"As soon as." Cyril tapped the desk with his knuckles. "As soon as."

***

Cyril had arranged to use the family liaison room for the interview with Crookson, an area that was less intimidating than the standard interview room. Crookson was alone as he sat having refused refreshment – he seemed eager to end the experience as quickly as possible. Cyril entered and placed a number of items on the table between them.

"Thank you for coming. I will caution you, not because of any wrongdoing but to ensure we are working with the truth on all matters. We shall also be recording this interview; the cameras are for your security as well as for ours. Your rights are explained in this pamphlet." Cyril pushed it across the table.

Rodney's leg bounced nervously as he rested a hand on his knee in an effort to calm it. "Can't say I've ever been in a police station, even as a kid. My father would have killed me had he been called to collect me from one."

"Times change. For your information we're following up a number of leads generated from your swift response in calling the police last night. If we can bring whoever is responsible into custody, we might prevent another death."

Crookson nodded. "Indeed. I didn't sleep too well I can assure you but I'm grateful you sent an officer last night and today to be with Jennifer. She seemed very nice. Lovely smile. It's true what they say, the older you get, police officers seem to get younger."

Cyril said nothing but he made a mental note.

***

April sat opposite Jennifer who stirred the teapot before slipping over a knitted tea cosy in the shape of a sheep.

"Are you married, April?"

April had immediately dropped the formality on arrival, first with Rodney. She needed to glean as much information as possible and she was aware the more formal the interview, the less likely she was to receive the information she required. She needed any barriers there might be to be lowered. April chuckled as if embarrassed. "Only to a Great Dane named Ralph. I've had the occasional male friends recently and a few longer relationships but this job is unforgiving when it comes to regular hours and stable relationships. That's why coppers tend to marry coppers, they understand the complexities and time constraints of the job. For how long have you been married, Jennifer?" April watched as she poured the tea.

"A long time! We met in '66, the year of England's World Cup win. My parents were in the wool trade, there were still mills in the major cities, can you believe. We owned one of the last. Modern loft style housing it is now, sadly. When my father sold that we moved away and Daddy bought a farm near North Rigton. We were still in the wool trade, sheep you see, hence ..." She pointed to the tea cosy. "I met Rodney at a cricket club dance organised by Daddy and Roger's family was there. I'd met him before but ... anyway, neither of us liked cricket so we just sat outside and chatted." She paused, looking wistfully towards the window. "He was quite the romantic with his beautiful manners, impeccable clothes and fancy car. We married in 1968, August. Initially, we had an apartment close to the shops but in the countryside between Leeds and Bradford until we found the house we wanted, which was this one. We still had the apartment until a year or so ago but there's not much countryside around it now."

"Remaining married for over fifty years is quite an achievement nowadays. Congratulations."

"People think it's easy but it's not. Sadly, we couldn't have children and I know Rodney would have loved to have a son to hand on the business to but as it happens, the clothing trade has faded rapidly over the last fifteen years what with the internet and online buying. The shops were sold one by one, the flat too. I had all the tests, as money was not an issue but ..."

"Could it not have been a problem with your husband's fertility? We women immediately blame ourselves."

"We had tests and discovered he had a low count, if you know what I mean, but he was, they said, capable of fathering a child but it might take time. They informed us it was probably the result of a serious allergy he had suffered when he was a youth. We tried, goodness we tried. He cut down on his drinking and stopped smoking cigars and even though we, you know, did it every other day, nothing happened. They said it might be his stress level." She poured the tea.

"It must have been stressful with Rodney looking after the shops and all the travelling."

"He had much to prove with changing the shops against his father's better judgement, believing they should target a younger clientele. But as I said, we had an apartment where he could stay if business demanded and if he didn't feel like driving home in the winter months in the dark. He called it his den. I'd occasionally stay there but not very often. I love my garden and the peace Harrogate offers although the last number of days have been a total nightmare." She sat back. The same look came into her eyes as April had previously witnessed. "I'm not naïve, April, I knew what might have been going on in the flat. I always knew he had an eye for the ladies and they loved him but to be honest, I had very little interest after not conceiving and as long as he came home to me—" She suddenly stopped. "I'm sorry, I'm rambling like my mother used to ramble and I promised myself I'd never get like her. She didn't like Rodney, I think she knew what I suspected. Rodney worked very hard and was very successful but he liked ... Sorry, there I go again."

"So, you do believe he had affairs?"

"No, not real affairs, dalliances, maybe, but affairs, no."

***

The photograph of Patricia Melling was positioned on the table in front of Rodney Crookson, then the photograph taken at the exhibition was placed alongside. "We thought the two photographs together might help jog your memory."

Crookson popped on his glasses. "That's Patricia at the exhibition. She'd not been with us long, she worked on Saturdays and occasionally in the holidays. When she went to college to become a teacher, she worked the Christmas and then Easter." He picked up the photograph of the woman and child but shook his head.

"We believe that to be Patricia and we know it would be close to autumn, 1972. We believe the child was conceived in 1972. At our previous meeting you suggested this photograph was taken in 1970. Was she still working for you in 1972?"

He nodded. "If my memory serves me correctly, she worked last around the time of the Easter holidays when she was back from college. She'd grown up, changed, she was less shy. She was going to work the long summer holidays too but she didn't. I don't recall why, it's a long time ago." Crookson's face flushed as he removed a handkerchief from his breast pocket.

"Did you ever have sex with any of your staff, Mr Crookson? Please remember, you have been cautioned."

There was a pause. Crookson's face contorted either in anger or angst; it was difficult for Cyril to discern which but he allowed the silence to weigh heavily as he watched Crookson bite his lower lip. He then saw him nod.

"This is recorded on video but it is far better if you answer as it saves any confusion and misinterpretation of your gestures."

"Yes."

"One or more than one?"

Crookson suddenly sat up as if he had found some inner strength and confidence. "Whenever the opportunity came my way if you really must know. I was young and healthy."

"And you were married at the time, I believe, from the records," Cyril collected the two photographs.

"Jennifer was indifferent, we couldn't have a child. It was possibly my fault but the specialists said differently. You see, I have a low sperm count; I was told it was to do with having a serious reaction to a tetanus injection when I was a teen. My parents didn't think I'd survive the day. I had to wear a medical alert medallion in case I had an accident and they tried to give me that vaccine again. Later, I was told, the injections for tetanus were produced by a different process and so, when I was older, I could discard it, the medallion I mean. I wore an identity bracelet, gold containing the same information; at the time they were quite trendy. I wasn't cavalier, Detective Chief Inspector, I always wore a condom. It wouldn't have been fair on Jennifer otherwise."

"Fair?" Cyril was surprised by the man's moral logic.

"If one became pregnant and she couldn't have a child. That would have been totally unacceptable."

"Did your wife ever suspect?"

"I think she had an idea. The bitch of a mother-in-law came to the flat one day and … well, I was compromised. From then on, she always had a face like a slapped arse when I was with Jennifer but whether she said anything, I'm not too sure."

"Patricia Melling. Did you have sex with her?"

***

April handed the photograph of Rodney standing with some girls at the exhibition in Harrogate. "Do you recognise anyone from this photograph?"

"Goodness me! That takes me back. We used to attend a good number of events like this. That's me in the background." A broad smile came to Jennifer's lips.

April leaned over and looked at the figure on which the finger rested.

"That, I believe, is a Saturday girl, and if you give me a minute … I think her name was Melling. She moved to Harrogate later in life when she married. Strange how I never bumped into her. She'd probably changed. Now, that young woman there is Lynda Checkley, she married a man who worked for Daddy, Jim Gough, a lovely lad. As I said, Daddy then had a farm. Goodness, they'll be in their eighties if God has spared them."

"Patricia Melling?"

"Yes, that's her. She stopped working at the shop when she was at college, if my memory serves me correctly. I can't recall the year. Rodney might remember. You could ask him when he comes back."

***

"Yes, she stayed late in the shop one evening, we were doing a stock take. I promised to take her home. She rang her mother to say she'd be late and that I'd be dropping her off."

"You had sexual intercourse?"

Crookson nodded.

"Yes or no, Mr Crookson?"

"Yes. She then seemed so upset afterwards. I realised it was her first time. She'd been at college away from home for six months so I never thought she'd still be … I remember she sat on the changing room floor and cried. I felt dreadful. I can assure you that I didn't force myself on her, it just happened as these things do."

"Did it become a regular thing?" Cyril took another photograph from a folder as he spoke.

"That's the thing, it was just the once. She came back for a few days. Unfortunately, we had a staffing issue and so I was at our Leeds shop and that was that. I received a rude note from her father to say she'd decided not to continue her temporary work."

"Did he say why?"

"No and I didn't ask. I sent her a thank you letter and some flowers but I heard nothing after that."

Cyril placed a colour photograph of a child aged about

five on the table. "As you know, this too was in the envelope you received."

"I remember seeing it there and I can truthfully say that I have no idea who that might be. All I know is it's not me." For the first time since being in the room a smile came to his lips. It was not reciprocated.

Chapter 21

April sat alongside Cyril and Owen.

"She didn't hide the facts but in some ways she seemed in denial about the extent of his philandering. His wife knew about his indiscretions. He had the perfect location, the apartment, it was 'his den'." She traced inverted commas in the air with her fingers. "He also wore a medical alert, possibly not dissimilar from the one found."

Cyril added. "Allergic to tetanus, just like Spencer. Strange coincidence but we can check from his medical records. Nobody has ever heard of it before and then two people in one investigation suffer from it. You might not be surprised to hear he had sex with Patricia Melling during her Easter break from college when she was working in the Bradford shop. He admitted to the one occasion and he used a condom. Funny how his memory is so focused."

April could not prevent herself from laughing. "Spontaneous lust but he just happened to have … tell that to the Marines, as my dad would say. From what I picked up from the conversation, his wife was frigid and therefore he got it wherever possible. Promotion, Miss Jones? Well, I just have to interview you first. We'll use the changing room. These people are in every walk of life, I believe – I've faced it but it's coming to an end. Just look how the #MeToo Movement has shaken the 'we're all boys together' brigade."

"The force is beginning to wake up to the issue of misogyny, too," Cyril responded. "It may be late for some but it's beginning to gather momentum, the past is starting to shake the establishment. Crookson clearly had no idea who the child was in this photograph, he was being truthful. I felt sure from his reaction he'd never seen him before. He's demonstrated his memory's been accurate, even down to the dates and the condoms, so I've no reason not to believe him at this stage." Cyril looked at April.

"We do have another name." April's tone became more upbeat. "One of the other girls in the photograph taken at the exhibition. This one." April's finger rested on the picture. "Lynda Checkley, now Lynda Gough, she's seventy-six and still with us. She has a cottage in North Rigton. I'm seeing her this afternoon. Her husband worked for Jennifer's father but he's passed away."

Cyril scrutinised the photograph. "Let's hope her memory is sharp too."

"So why does our possible killer hand over an envelope showing the faces of the three victims plus one of Melling and child? I can only assume the others images to be of the same child at various stages of growing up until about the age of twelve." April asked.

"The killer's the child?" Owen's first contribution to the conversation seemed to hit the nail squarely on the head.

"In one, Owen, in one. Could he be the adoptee and if he is, why kill three good folk?" Cyril looked at each person in turn. "If that's the case, we have revenge killings, wrongs are being put right and yet bizarrely, the three dead were all kind, charitable people; one was even the husband of the potential killer's mother, a man who stood by her and from all accounts cherished her. None of those murdered had children of their own or it's assumed they didn't." Cyril pulled a photograph to the front of the group. "It's this photograph that baffles me. Here the boy is about twelve and he's standing with a woman, a woman I believe to be Patricia. I know it's not yet been confirmed through forensic facial recognition tests but to me that's the same woman in the wedding photograph and others found at Spencer's house. Was Philip aware that they'd met, possibly on a few occasions, and had that caused some kind of problem?"

There was a pause. The rhetorical question hung in the air too long.

"So why the specific stamp?" Queried Owen.

April added, "Bleak Row, Gules House, Sepulchre Crescent. Remember what was interpreted from the writing left on Spencer's hand. It might be just as Shakti surmised, as this reinforces that it could, in a roundabout way, be linked to Dickens."

Cyril cupped his eyes with the palms of his hands and rubbed. Harry Nixon came into the room carrying a black handbag.

"Not your colour, Harry," Owen giggled.

"Not my bag, Owen." He placed it near Cyril. "Found after the search you requested, sir. Discovered in the shed beneath a number of items of clothing and blankets, hence the mold. Looking at the style of the bag it could be classed as retro." He looked at April for reassurance but none

191

came. Opening the bag, he tipped out a collection of photographs onto the desk. He also withdrew some gloves from his pocket. "There's probably not much Forensics will discover but I thought it a wise precaution."

"Spencer's house?" April asked. "I didn't think he had a shed."

"He doesn't. This came from Meredith's."

Slipping on a glove, Cyril turned the photographs to face the three of them. "That's Cole, a young Betty Cole." In her arms she was holding a child. "I'm presuming the child could be ... Fraser ... Fraser Melling." Cyril mumbled the names slowly as he went to a desk and collected a magnifying glass. He compared the photographs of the mother and baby taken originally from the envelope. "I think it's one and the same child."

"So, where was that taken?" Owen asked, trying to get a better look.

"It's on the back of the photograph along with a date, sir." Harry leaned forward and turned over the photograph. The words *Sepulchre Crescent* and the date 72 were written on the reverse. He turned over the others but they had only dates. 73, 75 and 80. There may be more at the house but as yet we haven't found them. We believe Meredith was the caretaker at the home but only much later, not when any of these were taken. He was in the military, remember, he was in the Falklands war in 1982 and he never let people forget it."

"So why would they be at Meredith's and why in a handbag? He wasn't married."

***

192

April stood before the whiteboard in the Incident Room. There was a general hum of conversation from those collating the strands of information coming in about this case in particular but some pertaining to the discovery at Kex Gill. She held a crumpled sheet of foil on which sat her lunch.

"Two men, both linked to the case, suffered from the same allergy to horse serum. And who said lightning couldn't strike the same place twice?"

"It hasn't," someone mumbled, "as they were not related."

April ignored the comment. *Both men knew each other in some capacity. DNA.* The thoughts came to her as she ate. *Could they be related? Could Spencer be a cuckoo in his family nest. If Rodney Crookson was a randy dandy could his father have been the same? Like father, like son?* She shook her head. Turning, she dropped the remnants of her lunch into the waste bin before looking at the images of Gules House just prior to demolition. It was in a sorry state. She believed most Victorian architecture had a certain style, an ornate grandeur, but this building had a disproportionate appearance, it was charmless and inhospitable … "In many ways it could be classed as 'Bleak'." Now she spoke out loud.

The photographs of Melling and the child were now displayed in chronological order. She had copies for her visit to Lynda Gough.

***

"It was a discovery waiting to happen, Owen." Dr Green spoke as he adjusted his bow tie in the mirror before running his fingers through his hair. Owen expected him to wet a finger and run it along his eyebrow but he was disappointed. "I received a call mid-afternoon. The surveyors were taking levels near the stream close to where it had been rerouted to travel underground; further subterranean routing is being planned, I believe, from our conversation."

"Not another set of remains." Owen thought of the proverbial that would hit the fan if they had to stop the work yet again.

Green shook his head. He moved to a computer at the far side of his office. Owen followed and looked at the screen, focusing on the single highlighted item. "How many guesses do I get?"

Green chuckled as he moved to a drawer to the side of the room. "You'll never guess as the items have naturally melded together and changed colour." He took out three objects. "On the screen you are looking at rubber gloves but they're not as sophisticated as these." He held them up before removing a small packet. He tore off the top before withdrawing a condom. "This is the important part." He put on the gloves and then held the condom before picking up a round pebble. "Imagine now the condom had been used and assume, for the moment, the killer was wearing gloves. You pull one glove from the hand trapping the condom and the pebble within the glove, then put that in the other hand and pull the other glove over both, thus trapping the items within two gloves. You toss the ball made up of gloves, condom and pebble into the stream to be carried well away from the crime scene just in case the body is discovered. They've not been in the water all this time but the ground where they were discovered was damp and peaty therefore helping to preserve what you see on the screen. The dark colour is leaching from the peat."

Owen leaned closer to the computer. "So that there is that?"

"Indeed, plus about fifty years' patina of course. We're hoping there may be some trapped DNA. Modern condoms and gloves tend to be biodegradable but fifty years ago? Like all things, they've improved. The gloves certainly would not biodegrade and therefore they formed a protective layer along with the peat."

"Can DNA be retrieved from that?" He pointed to the screen, the incredulity in his voice evident.

"Allegedly, they found a condom in Tutankhamun's tomb and traced his DNA in it, showing it to be used. I believe it was made from silk if you are interested. However, that, Owen, might be apocryphal but our scientists will work on it. It's a step closer, but don't hold your breath."

***

The village of North Rigton was off the main A658 Harrogate Road, linking the town with Pool in Wharfdale. It was quiet as April turned onto Brackenwell Lane. It was a lovely, rural setting. The sky seemed lighter and there had been no rain since lunchtime. The sun occasionally broke from the clouds, casting long shadows across the road. It made a change.

As she opened the gate, the front door opened. April moved quickly.

"Mrs Gough? I'm Detective Inspector April Richmond. Please call me April."

"Come in out of the cold, dear. The kettle's on. Take off your coat otherwise you'll not feel the benefit when you go back out. I saw you pull up. Did you find it alright?"

April slipped off her coat. "Yes, thanks to the Sat Nav. I appreciate your seeing me at such short notice."

"I was quite excited when you mentioned CC Fashions and Jennifer. I hope there's nothing wrong." She did not wait for a response. "Where does the time go? Tea?"

"Maybe a little later." April sat before the fire, it glowed red and Lynda gave it a poke. As the flames caught, they both felt the immediate warmth. The room was very much a time capsule but it was clean, ordered and homely. April glanced round for photographs but she saw none.

"How can I help you, love?" She moved the needlework she had been working on into a basket by her side. "Keeps the fingers and the mind active in the winter months."

April nodded. She had decided not to mention the murders, even though Lynda might have heard about them. She handed her the photograph taken at the exhibition.

Lynda smiled warmly as she identified the people within it and the moment captured came flooding back. "Goodness me! Where did you get this? Do you know, we had a lovely day. Do you know where this was taken?"

April nodded, enjoying the delight clearly etched on Lynda's face.

"Mr Crookson spared no expense. That's me, a young strip of a lass. That there is Marcia, we all thought she

196

looked like Lulu, the singer, but she was as musical as a stone trough. There's Patricia, it was so sad. She was so shy when she came to work Saturdays. We had a few young ones come and go, all lovely girls, like models they were. I don't think Mr Crookson would appoint an ugly one. I met Patty a few times. That's what I always called her. We became friends."

"Did you know why she left?"

"She went to college. She was going to be a teacher."

"Did you know she was pregnant the year after this was taken?"

Lynda nodded. "As I said, we were good pals, we confided in each other, talked about pop music and boys. She was made to give the child up. Did you know that? Her father was furious but once the child was gone, he seemed to warm to her again. She'd obeyed his order." She paused and shook her head. "It didn't matter how Patty felt. It seemed so wrong. Fortunately, she met a man who could love her."

"What was it like working for Mr Crookson?"

A broad knowing smile returned to Lynda's face. "Let's say he had a reputation. You were advised not to be trapped alone with him, wandering hands and other parts. Some girls actively encouraged him. He would take them out to a country club at Five Lane Ends in Bradford, I think it was called Moorlands. Big house in its own grounds. He'd wine and dine them. It had a casino and he always suggested they play cards and the like. He paid for their chips, you know, the things they gambled with. I heard they didn't come free, if you understand me, but the girls would never experience that type of lifestyle without his so-called generosity. Some of them were free and easy in many ways if you get my drift. Some called him Rodney the Rod." She blushed slightly.

"And Patricia?"

"She never said. She was a good girl and made a mistake but he could be very persuasive. He had a nasty side too. A few girls told me, if he didn't get everything he expected after he'd spent good money, he could turn very nasty."

"Aggressive?"

"No, just spiteful and churlish. Some staff just never returned and no reason was given. He'd soon find a replacement."

"When did you last see Patricia?"

Lynda frowned. "I saw her regularly. We were friends really until she died. Dreadful disease she had, a few people from there contracted it. Sorry, I didn't say but we worked together again years later at ICI Fibres in Harrogate and our friendship was rekindled. I just assumed you knew that, dear."

Chapter 22

Cyril walked into Meredith's backyard. The light was beginning to fade and the temperature was falling. The motorcycle was still in the shed; it was in a sorry state. Brian Smirthwaite had again searched the property but nothing of any significance had been found other than the bag. Cyril doubted the bag had been in the parcel he had collected from the Legion but he could not be certain. Richard Forsyth, the neighbour, pulled up in his van. He waved and moved to the gate.

"Lost something?"

"We're searching for something but for what we're not too sure, Mr Forsyth. Such is the nature of police investigation. Many people say a copper couldn't find his arse with his hand in his back pocket but I assure you that's not the case."

Forsyth laughed. "The old jokes are always the best."

"What we have found, however, poses more questions than it solves, hence our presence."

Forsyth frowned. "That reminds me. Give us a minute." Forsyth turned and dug his keys from the van before opening his garage door. He waved Cyril over. "When the bike and what remained of the sidecar had to go into the shed in more than two bits, he asked if I could store this for him until the bike was either fixed or sold. Neither of those plans came to fruition but I was left lumbered with this old tin chest."

Cyril just stared at the rust-coloured box. "Have you opened it?"

"Nope. There's not going to be a body in there is there? They've put spies in holdalls in the past so I'm sure, with a bit of effort, old Stan could get one of his old enemy from the Falklands in that!" He winked at Cyril before flicking on the garage lights.

Cyril opened the protesting lid of the box. On the surface were a number of old motorcycle magazines, some bike parts to the sides and near the bottom a large box file. Putting on some gloves, Cyril retrieved the file but in doing so, he disturbed one of the magazines. From between the pages fluttered a photograph. Forsyth picked it up. He frowned. "That's not the crafty old bugger with a child, is it?" He handed it to Cyril.

Cyril popped down the file and slipped on his glasses. "No." He immediately removed a magazine and flicked through it. Tucked well inside the pages were a number of items, from photographs to documents. Many had the telltale sign of once being stapled as the rust mark and the holes were clearly visible. The hairs on his neck seemed to stand on end as he began to realise, he had either found a treasure chest or a Pandora's box.

***

"Patty's mother-in-law worked at ICI and she got us both a job. It was unofficial and nothing special, cleaning and the like but it paid the bills. My Jimmy's health wasn't good and farming is not an easy way to earn a living, so we were grateful for what we could get. The social life linked with the firm was wonderful, they organised some smashing staff events, dances and such. Even did day trips out to the coast, all paid for and they didn't expect owt in return neither. Christmas was really special." She chuckled. "The bosses there were proper gentlemen."

April immediately hung on her last sentence ... 'Bosses were all gentlemen'. It was certainly a sign of the times when no women were in senior management roles.

"Patricia and Philip never had children. Do you know why?"

"After losing the little boy she said she couldn't, maybe it was the difficult birth. She told me she didn't get pain relief, the nurses told her it would teach her a lesson for her being too free and easy with the boys. It could also have been something in her head. When she'd had the child, those present told her to put it all behind her and think of the child rather than herself. I still can't think of that without getting cross. Put it behind you, for goodness' sake! Can you believe that? It wasn't as if she'd had her appendix removed, she'd had a child, her own flesh and blood. I suggested she get some counselling. Having another child would have made all the difference to her, I feel, but she didn't. She liked to see my kids. She'd have them round to hers for tea. Never forgot their birthdays until they were twenty-one."

"How well did you know Philip?"

"Well, but we only met socially at the ICI dos. He was a hard worker, grafter, worked for Hirst's, did a lot of travelling. He had a hidden side too, emotionally dark he was. Lovely man but I always thought there was something about him. There was a hardness. Some say it's a Yorkshire trait. It's difficult to describe really. I wouldn't have liked to be on my own with him for too long, we'd have had nothing to talk about once we'd mentioned the weather."

***

The box sat on the floor of the Incident Room. Spread on the tables were the motor cycle magazines. Nothing had been removed from them. On a separate table sat the box file. Cyril had organised for a photographer to be present who had set up video recording equipment in three different locations. Shakti, Harry and Brian were also present.

"The magazines are in the order in which they were removed from the box, looking from my left to right. There may be a time sequence that we need to keep and record. I'm assuming the older contents will be those lower in the chest and so trapped within these here." Cyril trailed his hand over the set of magazines. "They are of mixed dates and do not follow a chronological pattern. Nothing will be removed from between the pages but photographed, numbered and logged digitally so we can make up an order of the contents. Hopefully that will allow us to see if there's a time-line structure. The camera will project images onto the big screen so we can see the details more easily."

Gloved hands opened the pages of the first magazine until they came to an inserted item. If the item faced the incorrect way it was turned round. There were fifteen magazines in total and everyone knew they would be there for several hours.

The discovery was more time-consuming than expected. Each member of the team made their own notes as one by one the contents trapped within the magazines were checked, photographed and discussed. After two hours they were ready to start on the box file itself.

***

"Did Patricia ever see the child?" April sat back, away from the fire. She sensed there was a sudden reluctance to answer the question. April took out another photograph and handed it to Lynda. She said nothing but watched as Lynda studied it. As smile erupted across her face, her eyes became a mass of wrinkles.

"Will you see here. Goodness, that takes me back. I took that."

"Is that—"

"That's my Jo with Patty. That was taken in the garden here. The hedges have grown since then but you can see the tree."

"How many children do you have, Mrs Gough?"

She let out a laugh. "Well, that's another story. We thought we wouldn't have any but we got Jo and then the twins came along pretty soon afterwards. It was as if once we'd started, we couldn't stop. We've been blessed in a way. Jimmy says that happens a lot on the farm with the animals, one begets more."

"How old is Jo?" April immediately thought of the

homeless character who had known Philip and logged it mentally.

Lynda giggled. "Gracious me, how embarrassing. I think he's fifty-two, yes. Or is it fifty-three?"

"Is it short for Joseph?" April quizzed.

"Josh, Joshua but he likes neither. Just likes plain Jo."

April felt a sudden shiver as she heard the name. *Joshua, the leader.*

"Like his dad he is, he only likes Jimmy from me. It's Jim to everyone else.

"May I ask again, Lynda. Did Patricia ever see her child after it was given up for adoption?"

"She did, yes, but that possibly proved even worse for her mental state. Whenever she could. I remember Jo and the lad played in the park together on more than one occasion. She only had him for the odd hour or two and it was so irregular." Lynda handed back the photograph and collected her needlecraft. It was a sign. It was clear she had said all she wanted to. "I hope I've been some help. You never did have that tea."

"Did she have the baby at home do you know?"

"Mother and baby home, not a good place, like I said, the nurses were so cruel. Somewhere north. Richmond, I believe. It's no longer there I was told, thank goodness."

"We found postcards signed just 'F' and a note beneath flowers. 'Merry Christmas Mummy'."

Lynda smiled. "Really. That was kind of someone."

Slipping on her coat, April approached the door. On the wall was a framed tapestry. A circle containing a curved line through the centre splitting the black from the white and two contrasting dots in the upper and lower areas was displayed.

"Is this one of yours, Lynda?"

Lynda smiled. "I made it for my Jo. He loved it, said the symbol was like him and his best friend, one lucky, the other not, one dark and one light, happy and sad. He was into Kung Fu at the time and that was on his badge. Everybody was Kung Fu fighting. Remember the song? I used to sing it to Jo when he was little."

"Yin and yang," April whispered. "And was that true about his friend?"

Lynda just shrugged her shoulders. "Who knows what goes on in a lad's noggin. I did it a long time ago. I should send it to him. He lives away now. Hope it's not been a waste of time for you. Always good to reminisce." She opened the door.

"One more thing. Does Jo live locally?"

"You ask a lot of questions, don't you. As I said, he lives away."

"That's my job, Mrs Gough."

"Well, as it's your last, no, but local enough for me. He drives a taxi, used to have a wagon but business wasn't so good and he refused to go into farming."

April felt the atmosphere grow cold and she realised it was not only because they had moved away from the fire and the front door was open.

***

Cyril spread the items out one after the other. It was clear that many of the documents had been typed, some contained corrected errors. They too had signs of having something stapled at a corner. Some elements of each had been redacted. The name Gules House and the address were marked across the top.

"Bloody hell, that takes me back to when all the police reports were done on the old Olivetti typewriter, usually using one finger at a time," Brian said.

"Sweet Jesus!" Cyril chipped in.

"Indeed." Brian smiled. "I used to always say that. Thank goodness they invented correcting fluid."

"No, Brian, concentrate on the magnitude of evidence that's staring us in the face!" He looked at the handwritten signature on the bottom of each letter. Many were signed, B Cole.

It did not take long before they all understood at what they were looking. The reference numbers to the top right-hand corner of each note were similar to those seen on the reverse of many of the photographs.

"Someone's been playing God." Cyril looked round at each of his colleagues in turn. "The newborn were given out to parents desperate for a child and irrespective of the birth mother's wishes. There are no details of the child's real mother on any of these documents, just an individual letter." He flicked through. "Boy: name: K. Girl: name: P. There's even one for twins here," he pointed to the inserted sheet. "S and T."

There were no dates, nor any further details of the mothers. The redacted information Cyril assumed to be the details of the adoptive parents.

"Did nobody control this bizarre trade?" Brian tossed his pen onto the table, disgust clearly evident in his voice. "It's like a bloody cattle market!"

"They did, not too long after this place was demolished. Social services and accountability were fast becoming the norm but post-war, Brian, there was a need to get unwanted children fostered and into care; unmarried mothers were frowned upon in the home and in the church. Today there's a shortage of those willing to foster and even fewer wanting to adopt. I believe the younger the child, the easier the process. Maybe considering Betty Cole's commitment to charity, she believed she was doing the right thing by bringing stability to children who were not planned and maybe not wanted. The term illegitimate was seen as a stigma, one to be avoided at all costs."

"Or was she just following orders? Atrocities have been justified in the past through following instructions and not taking responsibility for your own actions." Shakti leaned on her elbows. She too was clearly troubled by what was before her. "I wonder when the last one left the building, what date?"

"Times change. Certain things done and said by our parents in their day would not be acceptable now. We can't judge the past by today's standards as we in the future will surely be judged by our children's children. Much of what I see about me today, isn't acceptable."

Chapter 23

April stood before the whiteboard, her overcoat still over her arm. She stared at the word she had written a number of days before, 'Joshua'. Taking a pen, she added beneath it – 'Jo Gough??? Fifty-two'. She then drew a line to the yin and yang pattern and then another to the name 'Fraser Melling'. *Is there a connection between you two?* It was a thought that seemed to recur. *Which one is bad and which is good?*

"Penny for them," DC Henry Jones whispered.

April shook her head. "Did anyone tell you you're like smoke?" She chuckled. "Facts, Henry, are hard to discern when you can't see the wood for the trees and that's commonly interpreted into police speak as sifting the truth from the lies."

"I came to find you as we have the information Flash requested: the single occupants in accommodation on the nights the murders were committed based on the strict criteria. We have three who paid cash on arrival, didn't leave their real address or no address at all and walked in off the street; more importantly they left their key card in the drop off area. Their email addresses were also false. We checked and we surprised one poor fella when we asked about his stay in Harrogate. He was on holiday in Greece." He handed April the list of names. "CCTV footage has been requested."

"I thought these days you always left a credit card in case you ran up a bill." April looked confused.

"They make exceptions, especially if it's late cash can still be king. Anyway, we have a Ben Costello, Peter Smith."

She laughed out loud. "There would have to be a Smith!"

"And Stuart Marsh."

She turned to look at Henry. "This could be three different people or one person checked in to three different locations?"

"But none came back for the night when Crookson met the chap on Duchy Road."

"So, why not?" wondered April."

"Unless he was local or knew it would be the last contact and left the area once the package had been handed over or the venue couldn't be bothered responding."

April tossed down her coat onto the desk. "Anything else on the ones who stayed?"

Henry shrugged his shoulders. "Nobody could remember the individuals but as soon as we have the CCTV footage, we'll have a better picture. One other thing, Flash wants a catch-up briefing at five."

***

The Incident Room was busy as Cyril entered. The chatter calmed rapidly as he stood at the far end of the room, the large wall-mounted screen behind him casting its usual blue hue.

"Sorry for the late request. Progress has been made owing to an unusual find at Stan Meredith's home. I'm not going to plough through it in detail now but I want to give you all a brief overview. I also know April has some thoughts on this and we may have a link to the possible killer thanks to the requests made to the hotels. Meredith had, in his possession, a considerable number of confidential documents we know came from the children's home or orphanage, Gules House. Remember we tracked this from the note written on Philip Spencer's hand, although initially, there was a degree of doubt. The documents reveal children were born at the home and then given up for adoption. It was, as I see it, a kind of clearing house of the illegitimate. There's nothing within the pages found that will allow us to track the mothers or the children. However, we may, thanks to modern technology and the fallibility of past redoubt techniques, be in a position to trace the adoptive parents but I've been assured that nothing is guaranteed."

A hand waved. "How many children are we discussing here, sir?"

"We have documents and photographs for twelve, plus other information but we think what was in the box may be the tip of the iceberg and it may be all that was saved. We also believe, yet may never know, that Meredith retrieved these from the mother and baby home prior to its demolition. He might not even have known the significance of the documents but as Owen pointed out, he and Cole knew each other both when he was, for a very short time, caretaker there and then afterwards. Rodney Crookson also knew him, having seen him at Cole's house on more than one occasion. Mary, the niece, saw him too and remembered a number of details about him. They may have been just friends but we can't rule out a more in-depth involvement. I don't like presumption without facts but I'm prepared to make an exception right at this moment owing to other information that's come to light. I have a feeling one of the children put up for adoption in this process is the person for whom we search, the killer. What we do know is we're looking for a male."

April stood and moved next to Cyril.

"Two things. We have a possible connection to three male suspects staying in hotels, who met the criteria we set. We have found the process to be successful in past cases. No females were mentioned. There's a possibility that the three names are one and the same man and we'll have a greater understanding when the CCTV footage from the areas and the hotels is assessed. We're looking at twenty-four hours before that is released. Interestingly, there was no response regarding the latest attack, if you could call handing over an envelope an assault. We haven't traced anyone in a hotel or lodgings for that night. This might be due to its being the last job, revenge having been served and the perpetrator having now left the area."

Cyril interrupted. "That does make sense as nobody meeting the description was traced that evening even though a number of people were stopped. Sorry, April. Please go on."

"Today I met with Lynda Gough, formerly Lynda Checkley. She was identified from the photographs as being at the exhibition in 1970 along with Patricia Melling. I managed to have a chat, I wanted it to be informal and it was. She has three children, the first born is Jo." She moved to the whiteboard and tapped the name she'd written earlier. "I've added the connections that immediately came to mind. Joshua, her son only liked to be known as Jo. The significance of that will not be lost on you all as Joshua led his people to the promised land!" She looked around to ensure her comment had been understood. "You'll know the homeless donor of stamps to the charity shop was also known as Jo. Was this one and the same person? Secondly, one of his favourite symbols when he was younger was this, yin and yang and we know the significance within this case, the link to Cole's murder. More importantly as far as I'm concerned, was the fact she knew Patricia was pregnant, had given birth in a place for unmarried mothers and had passed on the child under her father's firm instructions. Yet she met the boy, her son, occasionally. Apparently, she told me both Joshua and the boy played together." She paused.

"Did Lynda name the other boy, Patricia's son?" Shakti's question brought a shake of the head.

"No, and I decided at that moment not to ask. I'll be seeing her again, however. Lastly, it is apparent that Rodney Crookson had a dreadful reputation as a womaniser. He was manipulative, a bully, misogynistic and cruel in his attitude towards younger and more innocent members of his staff. You could say, like the symbol here, he was black and white. If you were co-operative, so was he. I'd like to pay him a visit and take Owen with me, as usually Owen's physical presence brings a stabilising influence to tricky interviews."

"Or you could request he attends the station again," Cyril suggested whilst straightening the papers before him.

"Home is less intimidating, sir."

"I'll organise that," Shakti responded having difficulty keeping a grin off her face.

"Thanks everyone. A reminder to keep an open mind. As soon as we have anything from CCTV or details of what has been redacted from the documents we now have, you'll all be informed." Cyril tapped April on the shoulder. "Well done!"

***

The walk home from the police station seemed endless. The darkness conspired to work in concert with the hanging mist bringing a greater depth of cold. Already frost had layered the vehicles parked by the side of the road, cloaking them with an ethereal glow to the upper surfaces. The flashing lights of a gritting wagon came into view before passing and broadcasting a fine sheet of particles across the carriageway. Cyril turned up his collar. On evenings like this he wondered why he walked. *Come on, Bennett, it's good for you, clears the cobwebs and keeps the waistline in check.* He had refused lifts so often that no one offered any longer.

Robert Street was a welcome sight and within minutes his key was in the lock. The immediate heat embraced him as he entered and the smell of cooking brought a calming rumble to his stomach. He had forgotten how hungry he was.

"Did you have a good day?" Julie's voice made the trial of the walk so worthwhile.

"It is now." He leaned into the kitchen. "Smell's delicious."

"It'll be ready in thirty minutes if you want to shower and get some drinks."

Cyril did not need asking twice.

Cyril had been at the table some time as he moved the risotto around in the bowl before sprinkling on some parmesan cheese and adding black pepper.

"You've not tasted it and you're adding pepper!" Julie knew he would, she chuckled but seeing his expression stopped abruptly. He was clearly troubled. Putting down her cutlery she slid her hand and rested it on his. "You can talk to me. I know both cases are difficult but I suspect one—"

Cyril did not let her finish, neither did he look up until he had put his other hand on hers. "Children were taken from their mothers within hours of birth. People, strangers, were lined up ready to take them. We don't know as yet if there were a vetting procedure or who selected the prospective parents."

Julie looked into his eyes and could see the depth of his distress. She wanted to just hold him but she knew it would eat at him the whole evening unless they brought it out in the open. "It shocks me too. When you mentioned it before I couldn't help but do some digging and I'm sure you and the team have too. There was a major scandal of forced adoption in the 50s 60s and 70s where not only the church and charities colluded to remove children from unmarried mothers, but the government also. This practice not only reached all corners of the United Kingdom but was rife in

Canada and Australia too. At the birth, certain unmarried mothers were flagged which meant their child was going for adoption irrespective of the potential for psychological harm. There's a government report, you'll know it. 'The Violation of Family Life. Adoption of Children of Unmarried Women 1949–1976'. It's a scary read. Even with better provision of contraception, abortion and welfare payments after these dates there is a belief this poor practice still continued."

Cyril nodded and forced a smile recognising her support. He squeezed her hands. "April has, I believe, reviewed that document and was disgusted, like us all, by her findings. It's hard to comprehend this could have ever happened, to consider it right or proper. The report, I'm informed, reveals that young girls were punished for their pregnancies, made to scrub steps and when they reached the bottom they went back to the top. They were not given adequate pain relief as a way of teaching them a lesson for their immorality. People like Betty Cole believed she was doing the right thing, helping in some misguided belief that both the mother and the child would benefit, the child would not carry the stigma of illegitimacy and the family of the girl would not have to face the shame the pregnancy brought. The evidence is beginning to suggest that one of those children, and possibly one of the last to go through this system, is now responsible for the deaths of the three victims. However, Philip Spencer's murder is an anomaly. His wife was one of the young women who suffered this dreadful abuse and he was, from all accounts, charitable and kind, whereas Meredith and Cole were involved in the home at certain times." He sipped some wine. "It's hard to understand the logic of revenge if logic exists at all. Anyway, that's for tomorrow. Thanks for your involvement. It's going to be a sad one whatever the outcome."

Chapter 24

Surprisingly, Rodney Crookson had been affable when the interview was suggested and he was quick to offer a time. Although there was a heavy frost that morning, there was a hazy, low sun and even though it did contrive to make driving eastward difficult, it was more welcome than the grey skies to which they had recently become accustomed. The traffic through the town centre was unusually heavy and as the car turned down Duchy Road Owen dropped the sun visor and squinted. "Bloody hell! Blinded by the light!"

As they parked April looked at Owen and made the sound of a bell ringing.

"Round one and in the red corner ..." She never let her face slip as she collected her belongings and left the car. Owen followed.

"I'll bring a towel. I may need to chuck it into the ring when either you or he surrenders"

April just pulled a face.

The garden looked beautiful with its frozen, glittering coat. She paused and admired the crystal uniformity sprinkled so accurately on every surface. "Isn't nature just wonderful, Owen."

"Aye, unless you're up at silly o'clock like I was scraping nature off the windscreen. My hands were like two cubes of ice. Wonderful, yes, if you say so."

Before they had reached the door Rodney opened it, allowing them to enter quickly. He was pleased to see it was the young female detective whom he immediately recognised. He studied Owen and watched as he instinctively lowered his head when entering even though there was ample clearance.

"Did you bring your bodyguard with you today?" Rodney's comment was ignored. "Thank you again for looking after Jennifer the other morning. Do go through into the sitting room. Dreadfully cold morning but the frost looks so majestic on days like these when the sun catches the myriad crystals don't you think." His poetical comment was deliberately aimed at her.

April looked at Owen and mouthed the words, 'See' followed by 'Philistine'.

"Before we begin, may we offer you a hot drink and maybe a biscuit?"

Immediately he now had Owen's full attention. "Thank you, tea, white, one sugar."

Rodney smiled and left them briefly. When he returned he said, "Jennifer will bring it shortly."

"I would like this interview to be without your wife's presence as it is of a sensitive nature. However, should you wish her to hear all we have to say, she's welcome to stay." April was matter-of-fact.

Rodney frowned but nodded. "I see. Do go on."

Jennifer entered, poured the tea and left. "Please ask if you need more." She looked at Owen as he leaned over, took a sugar lump from the pot, popped it in his mouth before adding two more to his tea; the sugar tongs remained unused.

Initially, the interview was very one-sided as April detailed the information she had received from Lynda Gough. Crookson sat back and listened, allowing little to no expression to form. He neither contradicted nor supported any of the accusations voiced. However, when Moorlands Country Club was mentioned he sat forward in his chair.

"Goodness, I'd forgotten about Moorlands. It's no longer there, in fact, much of Five Lane Ends has changed beyond recognition. I was a young man, the opportunities were there and all the ladies were, as far as I knew, consenting adults. Let me add this: not only does the physical environment change, the buildings and the like, but so too does society. The sixties and seventies were very different, they were free and progressive but neither of you would know that. They were special times and you had to live through the period to understand that fully. My parents had witnessed dark times with the wars and rationing but the sixties and seventies, well it was like spring after the coldest of winters. I was not alone. Many of the ladies were promiscuous, enjoyed a good time, loved to be wined and dined. They were not children, Detective Inspector. They were swinging times, peace and love."

He sat back and April could see his confidence grow as he looked first at her and then with greater assurance at Owen.

"Correct me if I'm wrong but I don't believe I broke any laws, criminal laws, that is. Personally, and some might say morally, I bent some rules. I also understand that, viewed now, my actions could be construed as unacceptable. It's always easy to judge from afar when we stand on what is believed to be a high moral ground and because it's simple, it serves no purpose, it's irrelevant. We've all judged our parents, old fashioned ways, not enough progress, not enough change but at the time, nobody was harmed. What do they say now … nobody died because of our actions, my actions."

April glared at Crookson and thought of the three dead.

"And yes, they were not only my actions. These ladies were not dragged kicking and screaming into the restaurants or indeed into my bed. They came happily and willingly and many were thrilled to be there on many occasions. The fact you wanted Jennifer sheltered from this conversation suggests you feel she's unaware of my sexual past but then you'd be wrong. She's very much aware of the past, my past and therefore her past. We have no skeletons hidden in these cupboards if you're hoping in some devious way to expose them."

"So, Mr Crookson, you never forced yourself on these women even though you were in a position to hire and fire?" It was the first time Owen had spoken.

"Some ladies did not enjoy working in the shop, you would naturally see employees come and go. We took on more staff at key times of the year, Christmas was always a busy time, Easter and summer. It was ever thus. Especially so when my father wasn't running the shops."

"Mary Bailey worked for you, another Saturday employee, another young girl just like Patricia Melling. She was your neighbour's niece, I believe."

"She did and we're still friends. As you know she's next

door performing the difficult task of sorting out her aunt's estate."

"Why did she stop working for you?" Owen leaned forward forcing Crookson to sit back. "She worked in the Harrogate shop, I believe. Her aunt asked if you needed a Saturday girl."

Rodney nodded. "The young folk move on; the jobs are just that, temporary. They have educational commitments. I believe she found a job in Skipton that was more to her liking. She lived there but I'm sure you're aware of that."

"No card and flowers then like when Patricia Melling left?" April asked.

"Just what are you insinuating?" Rodney bristled.

April continued. "The interview you had with DCI Bennett clearly states you had sexual intercourse with Melling and she left your employment. I'm trying to establish why Mary followed suit."

Owen leaned forward and took another sugar lump. "You don't mind?" He looked directly at Crookson as he held it between his finger and thumb.

"No, help—"

"What happened when you took her home?" April demanded. "I believe it was only the one occasion."

"Just what has she been saying? It's a long time ago."

Neither April nor Owen spoke for a moment.

"I'm going to caution you and ask that question again," April informed him.

Within minutes she saw Crookson retrieve a handkerchief from his breast pocket, wipe his eyes as he continued.

"Mary felt travel sick and I stopped. I'd been driving too

fast, showing off, I suppose. I pulled up at the bottom of Kex Gill as it was the only safe stopping place. She went into the woodland next to the layby. I thought she might be … Anyway, I followed her. I was extremely foolish. You might not believe me but I regretted that I interpreted something that wasn't there."

Owen stared at the man opposite and slowly popped the sugar lump onto his tongue. "If she or any of your staff were to decide to make an official complaint of sexual abuse, sexual harassment, especially if it's linked to the workplace, no matter how far back they want to go, then we will be obliged to investigate those allegations formally. From what we know so far, there is ample evidence to make life very difficult for you both emotionally and, depending on the outcome decided by the courts, possibly financially. The press would have a field day. Once the allegations become public knowledge, it's remarkable how many people come out of the woodwork. Revenge, as the saying goes, is best served cold and many of the co-operative women of whom you speak might have a different idea of what really occurred, especially when the idea of compensation comes into the equation."

Crookson's whole demeanour had changed. The confidence and degree of arrogance had evaporated and an old man, confused and hurt, now sat before him. He was a shadow of his former self. Owen glanced at April and then back at Crookson.

***

Owen had been back some time when he briefed Cyril

about the interview before moving through to the kitchen. He needed a brew. Returning to Cyril's office he placed the cup and saucer on the desk, put down his mug and poured what had slopped in Cyril's saucer back into the cup.

Cyril looked at Owen, the cup and then at Brian. "Doesn't Brian get a brew?"

"I only have two hands."

Cyril shook his head and looked at the CCTV images on screen that had come from the hotels. Gait analysis had established that the three people were in fact one and the same. However, the person did look very different in the various shots.

"We have established an approximate height of 5ft 10 to 11. We also have tracking images in four locations in town for two of the dates." Brian moved the video on. "This is the best facial image we have but the scarf and the hood conceals so much."

"Enhance what you can, Brian. Run them against people we have marked on the boards."

April popped her head round the door. "I've had a call from Mary Bailey, I left her my card. Crookson's been round after the meeting we had. His mood was not happy. From what I believe, Andrew, her husband, has punched him."

Cyril closed his eyes. "That man is bloody high maintenance. Owen, go with April. Imagine you're treading on eggshells. Get him out of the house so you can hopefully get the two sides of the story."

***

On arrival at Betty Cole's house, grey smoke was rising

from an old metal garden incinerator positioned on the driveway between the house and the garage. Small pieces of grey, charred paper thrown up by the focused heat were slowly cascading close to the road, like snow.

"Looks like they've announced a new Pope too as well as having a brawl, Owen."

"Looks like they're clearing out more like." He raised an eyebrow.

Crookson was sitting on the bottom step of the stairs. The light was on in the hallway. His nose had stopped bleeding but the handkerchief held on his lap told the story. Andrew had brought out dining chairs and positioned them facing him but neither was occupied. Owen leaned with his back against the front door as April let her gaze drift between Crookson and Andrew Bailey. Mary was standing down the hall, her arms wrapped tightly around her as if forming a physical barrier to all that was before her.

"I didn't strike him," Andrew immediately protested, "I just tried to keep him away from Mary. As God is my witness, I didn't strike him. His nose just started to bleed, probably owing to his highly confused state of mind when he came charging in here like a man possessed." Andrew pointed to a key on the floor. "He used that to enter through the back door. He kept shouting obscenities at my wife whilst trying to get close to her. What should—"

"No, no, I know what this is all about. It's about compensation, reparations. People swim in the same water for years without a worry and then one day they suddenly decide to complain that it's been too cold all that time they've been swimming. You see them on the news, 'He abused me twenty years ago and I'm a mental wreck'. It's all to do with compensation," Crookson grumbled, his voice remaining relatively calm. "We all have secrets, we all should know when to keep our mouths closed, especially at times like these when her dear aunt and my close friend has been so cruelly taken." Rodney dabbed his nose again and checked to see if it was still bleeding. "So, I touched the clothing over her tits a lifetime ago. She wasn't the total innocent, she had encouraged some sexualised banter, jokes and the like when we were in the shop together but that will have been conveniently forgotten. On that day, for some reason, she wanted me to take her home, she asked me and now she's come running to you." His finger waved between Owen and April.

There was a pause. Nobody spoke as they could see he had not finished saying what he had to.

"Look, the stress I've been through these last few days, in fact the stress and worry I'm still going through, has brought me to this emotional precipice. I'm sorry, Mary, I shouldn't have come barging in. I'm sorry for my unacceptable language and for any distress caused. I acted totally out of character but I was so cross that you'd brought this up at such a dreadful time."

"I asked you to take me home because my aunt was unavailable and my father was ill. You knew that." Mary's voice was shaking.

Andrew regarded April and then directed his eyes to the key on the floor. "And if I'd not been here, what then?"

The question was relevant. "Is that your key, Mr Crookson?" April pointed to the object even though it was clear for him to see.

He nodded. "Betty gave it to me years ago. She has a

key to our house as well just in case. It's what responsible neighbours do."

"Did you use that the morning you found Betty?" April moved and sat on one of the chairs before him.

"No, the back door was ajar. The key is kept in my safe. I was walking the dog so why take Betty's key with me? Had her door been closed and locked then I'd have dashed home for it."

You still could have on that morning and we only have your word for what truly happened, Owen thought. He stared at Crookson. He had seen so many of his character traits in such a short period of time that he felt as though he were looking at a chameleon.

April moved down the hall to Mary and ushered her into the kitchen. Mary paused, looking at a bottle on the table positioned near a collection of papers and some photographs. April could immediately see anxiety in her expression.

"What is it?" April turned Mary to face her.

"That bottle wasn't on the table, wasn't in the kitchen this morning before he came in."

As April moved to the table, she could not help but notice one of the photographs. She immediately identified Betty Cole holding a child. Deliberately saying nothing, she returned to the stairs.

"You came here today with the key and what else, Mr Crookson?" April's tone was direct but she immediately identified the puzzled look on his face.

"Nothing, just the key … and I returned a gift that we received from him, a bottle of wine." He looked at Andrew.

She moved to Owen and whispered an instruction. He

slipped his hand in his pocket, retrieving a nitrile glove and a forensic bag before moving towards the kitchen. As he entered, Mary was coming back in through the back door. The bottle stood alone on the table. Using his phone, he photographed the bottle in situ before slipping it into the forensic bag and taking it to the car. The incinerator was well alight as flames danced through the small metal chimney positioned on the lid. He went back into the hall.

"It's secure and in the car."

April returned to the kitchen. Mary was leaning against the table. The sheets and photographs had gone. "The papers, Mary?"

"Burning. My aunt squirreled away so much stuff that went back decades. It has to go."

The change in her was remarkable. It seemed as though she had gone from one end of the spectrum to the other within a matter of minutes.

"I'm sorry to have called you, Detective Inspector, but I was scared, not only for me but for Rodney. Andrew might have hurt him had he not had the nose bleed. I think he's learned a lesson. As I said before, I would never press charges for what happened years ago and as this is in some way linked to that, I just want it to be forgotten. If I may remind you, I did ask you not to mention to him what I revealed when we had our chat. It's clear, from what occurred here today, you used that against my wishes and that may well have been the catalyst that brought this about."

"So, you don't want to press charges is what you're now saying? And the key and the bottle?"

"The key sounds logical, I may have been mistaken

about the bottle, after all Andrew brought wine with him. He gave one to Jennifer as a thank you for some scones she brought round. Rodney might, in his anger and haste, have returned it. I didn't know that. I'm sorry if we've wasted your time."

***

"Dr Green's been pestering to chat with you, Owen. Called three times over the last couple of hours." Brian tossed a note onto his desk. "His number's there."

Owen looked at the note as he put two fingers into the mug positioned on his desk and withdrew an Uncle Joe's Mint Ball. Popping it into his mouth he dialled.

"You're very elusive today, Owen. I have two words for you, my friend, Deoxyribonucleic acid, or to the man in the street, DNA, the acronym that is music to our ears. They've managed to extract a sample from our Russian doll of rubber found at Kex Gill. All you need to do is find a match."

Owen stopped crunching the mint. "Music indeed from the men who are truly magical. Let's hope we can. Thank you."

"Remember, this is an old sample and is extremely sensitive. It's a guide, a signpost maybe, but at least it's something."

"And seeing the National DNA Database wasn't launched until 1995 our man might also be in the ground."

Chapter 25

"They were not dissimilar to those found at Meredith's, typed sheets and black and white photographs. I saw one photograph and I'm sure it was Cole holding a very young child. What was strange, from being very distressed, Mary had soon removed them into the incinerator when I left the kitchen, she'd also changed her tune regarding the bottle. The transformation in her character was remarkable."

Cyril picked up the frame containing the photograph of Liz Graydon. He remembered her steely determination and her total hatred of bullshit, no matter from where it emanated. "Have we been played, April? Have we smelled bullshit and thought it was roses?"

"I don't follow, sir."

"Consider your meeting with her when she disclosed Crookson's sexual advances."

April reflected as Cyril placed the picture frame back on the cabinet.

"One minute I was in a beautiful car and feeling grown up and special and then … I remember she went on to describe how he followed her. She said that he started to rub her back but then his hands moved gently round and found her ... breasts. It was the word 'gently' that I remember, it made me think at the time, it stuck out like a sore thumb; such a strange adverb to use in the description of an assault." April frowned.

"You're right, April. Maybe the young lady wasn't as innocent as she made out to be. Guilt can bring about fear and that, as we know, can make people strangers to the truth. As Crookson said, it's water that's long passed under the bridge. She also specified that she didn't want you to mention the conversation to him. Did she perhaps protest a little too much?"

April felt uncomfortable. Mary had been acting strangely from the moment she had arrived.

"If she'd been traumatised by Crookson why not just ring 999 – unless she wanted you specifically. You only knew of their past from that interview. She asked you not to mention it and therefore placed you between a rock and a hard place, knowing full well you could not grant her request."

"Do you think we might have Crookson all wrong?"

"Maybe, but from where we stand and with the evidence we have, he's just a philanderer, or he was. Right now, he's just a confused old man."

Brian Smirthwaite knocked on the open door.

"I hope you're the bearer of great joy, Brian," Cyril mumbled as he took his seat behind his desk.

"Forensics found a hair in the envelope that was handed to Crookson, one with a root which makes it even more exciting for the forensic scientists. As you know, we took samples from Spencer's house, concentrating on what we believed belonged to Patricia. He kept much of her things including her hair brush. What they've found, is a mitochondrial link. It's highly likely that the person who handed over that envelope is Patricia's son, the lost son. It is then probable he could also be the killer."

"Joshua Gough. We really must find him even though he's not missing. He seems to be coming onto our radar more and more. Let's put him through the system. If he is, as she said, operating a taxi, it should be relatively straight forward to locate him, Brian."

Within fifteen minutes Cyril's phone rang.

"It's all here. North Yorkshire Council Taxi Drivers and Operator's application and renewal forms. We have all the details, address, phone, registration and number as well as an up-to-date photograph. He's based in the Thirsk area. I've done a swift, personal check. He's divorced, no children according to the records."

"Thanks, Brian." Cyril checked his watch, shook his wrist and looked again. "Send through his personal details and a copy of the photograph. If we stop him, I want our people to know it's him and not a mate moonlighting."

Cyril put a call in to Control giving Gough's details. The digital file would follow. Initially, he needed ANPR records of the last seven days for the taxi and any other vehicles registered to him or to his address. There was, he knew, always the possibility he had booked taxi friends to bring him to Harrogate on the days the murders took place. Once he had exhausted that avenue, he would seek an arrest.

***

Owen had received the information regarding the discovery

of the DNA within the envelope. *Was the son confronting the father, the one responsible who had disappeared leaving a young mother and a child to fend for themselves? But if there were a need for revenge why just hand the images over and leave, after killing previously?* It did not make sense. As the thoughts tumbled in his head, the sensitive information brought back his own difficult childhood. His memories, however, were of gratitude, of laughter and security but he knew things could have been so different. Yin and yang, it all came down to fate. "If we find the son, we find the father," he mumbled to himself.

He checked back in the case file focusing on the DNA deposits at the three crime scenes. He recalled there was a greater concentration of a matching sample at Spencer's house. He now officially asked the question and awaited the response based on the new DNA information. The computers would soon find any link.

His mind switched to Crookson. In some ways he felt a degree of sadness for the old man. Finding the body had brought with it what seemed like the riders of the Apocalypse galloping across his Axminster. The significance of what that actually meant he had forgotten but he remembered Cyril mentioning them once in a case and it sounded frightening. He picked up the phone and dialled April's direct number.

"Hi, April. Do we have Crookson's DNA on file?" He could have checked the database but wanted to hear from April.

"We should have as he was in Cole's house after the murder and a sample would be required to eliminate him from the investigation. His prints were definitely taken, that I know for sure. Give me a minute."

Owen could hear her tapping the keyboard. "We do, yes. Confirmed. They are presently checking those on the bottle left on the kitchen table but that will take a while. Why?"

"There was a suspicion that he might be the father of Patricia Melling's son but if there's not a match found at the other crime scenes then it's highly unlikely. Nothing has come back from the hair DNA so far. If there had been a DNA profile fifty percent similar then we'd have confirmation he was the father."

Owen heard her sigh.

"You know every new sample taken is automatically checked on the DNA database. If there had been a match we'd have been informed immediately. So, you're correct, Owen."

"You sound disappointed."

"No, in some ways I'm just pleased for Jennifer. She's had a lot to put up with and still carries her burdens. Always remember, a tiger never changes its stripes." April waited for a response but none came.

As soon as Owen put the phone down it rang. It was Harry Nixon.

"According to Green we have a tentative positive on the latest ancient sample found at Kex Gill."

Owen leaned forward waiting for the information. "Come on, Harry, spill the beans, who is the tentative positive?"

"Rodney Crookson." Harry heard an involuntary whistling sound as if air was forced through Owen's tight lips.

"Bloody hell. She was right, a tiger certainly doesn't

change its stripes."

"Sorry?"

"Never mind, can we assume a tentative positive is definitive?"

"No, but it's the best you're going to get. Considering the success rate of obtaining a profile from a relatively recent semen sample is about seventy percent, it's near impossible to match this from a sample that's older than us, I don't think there's the accuracy we would like, or that would hold up in court but it's what we have. It's another important piece of the old jigsaw. It's what's done with the result that's important. Remember the man in the street believes any DNA link is accurate."

Owen scratched his head. Harry was right. The thought of what he could do with the result was what was important. It brought a smile.

Chapter 26

Cyril, April and Stuart Park approached the front door, Crookson's door, a door they had, over the last few days, now come to know better than their own. Jennifer opened it with a degree of caution, her facial expression revealing the strain she had been under and the renewed anxiety their visit caused. She focused her attention on April, a face she knew and a person she trusted.

"Has Mary made an official complaint, April?" she muttered, moving her hands to her mouth in anticipation of the answer she feared.

April moved in first and rested a hand on her shoulder. "No, she hasn't but we do need to talk to your husband. I have an assurance that neither Andrew nor Mary will be making any official complaint. They understand the strain you've both been under. Maybe we should make some tea whilst Detective Chief Inspector Bennett chats with Rodney."

"Tea, yes and maybe a scone. I made some … I think." She began to sob. "Rodney is in the lounge. He was asleep when I last looked."

Cyril tapped lightly on the architrave surrounding the

lounge door but did not wait for a response. Rodney was still asleep, his mouth agape. An occasional snore seemed louder than the rest. Cyril placed three photographs on the coffee table, the same coffee table he had used before and sat back. Park stood by the door. He was holding a notepad and pen.

Instinctively, Crookson's eyes opened and he focused on Cyril. "Bloody hell, not you again!" He rubbed his eyes and blinked heavily as if trying to purge the apparition before him.

Cyril spoke slowly.

"You do not have to say anything, but it may harm your defence if you do not mention, when questioned, something which you later rely on in court. Anything you do say may be given in evidence."

"Am I being arrested for the trouble I caused next door?"

Cyril shook his head. "Not yet. Please look at the photographs on the table before you. Do you know or recognise any of them?"

Rodney rubbed his eyes before slipping on his glasses. He picked up each photograph in turn, then quickly placed them back on the table. When he had scrutinised each one, he looked at his hands and then at Cyril. There was an inordinately long pause.

"I knew this day would come and yet the longer it took, the more I believed nothing would be revealed or said." His voice was weak and tremulous. "When I heard they were building the new road to alleviate the problems at Kex Gill I grew anxious. Jennifer, bless her, noticed the change in me. She's been a wonderful wife, understanding and bloody tolerant. I could not have wished for a kinder lady." He looked back down at the table and then at Cyril. "I regretted each one of these. The lad, of course, was a mistake." He laughed nervously whilst shaking his head. "Having long hair on a day when there was poor visibility." He leaned forward and tapped one of the photographs. "She was so co-operative. I was going to let her live but … I really don't know what drove me to do it. It was like a drug, an aphrodisiac. Once the Yorkshire Ripper started his killing spree, I hoped if the bodies were found the police would immediately believe they were just more of his victims."

Cyril continued to remain silent and was amazed to see Crookson sit up straight as if a huge weight had been removed from his shoulders.

"How did you know?"

"DNA. A condom wrapped in a pair of gloves."

Crookson laughed, a short, snort-like laugh that conveyed defeat and surrender. "That's so hard to believe but from what we see on the television these days, I can understand how that is now possible even after all this time. Maybe I've just lived too long. If I'd died sooner or the council had not decided to go through with the bloody road, nobody would have been any the wiser … It would only have continued to weigh on my conscience but then I've carried it for so long, a little longer for Jennifer's sake would have been a good thing, a blessing. Fate can be cruel as well as kind, Detective Chief Inspector, but you'll understand that doing the job you do."

Rodney spent a few moments focusing on different parts of the room and then back at Cyril.

"I think I'd like to go now. I'm ready. Living life under a shadow, living a lie for so many years has taken its toll. All I ask is that you'll leave that lovely lady to look after Jennifer like you did last time, I know she likes her. I'd hate to think of her here alone at this time."

"We will." Cyril turned to Park who helped Rodney from his seat.

"Someone wiser than I once said, 'Regret is a form of punishment itself'. I've had regrets for many years and been emotionally punished but hopefully now I'll find some peace. I just pray for Jennifer that she will find strength."

As Rodney was leaving, he collected a small photo of his wife from the sideboard, looked at it before slipping it into his pocket. Park looked at Cyril who nodded that it was acceptable. He thought of the picture of Liz Graydon he had hidden away for too long and knew the comfort it would bring. If the photograph would help a desperate man through the ordeal he was about to face, he could take it.

Cyril felt the churn in his stomach. He really did not like the person standing before him but he felt a degree of compassion.

Chapter 27

"Silver Skoda Octavia. We have ANPR records showing the car in a variety of locations until five days ago and after that nothing. It's either running on false plates or not running at all. My guess is it's parked or garaged," Dan announced.

"His address?" Owen muttered as he read through the list of locations.

"Checked and there's no car. The neighbours haven't seen it for a while or him. Its last known location was …" DC Dan Grimshaw gave the position. "That's some distance from his home and prime for routing along a number of minor roads."

"If all this was planned, he'd be aware of the ways we could track him down."

"We're checking credit card and phones registered to his address. Again, people who are organised will use a temporary phone or none at all, as well as using only cash. We saw that with the hotels. He's gone to ground."

April looked at the whiteboard. "I'll pay Lynda Gough another visit. If Joshua is involved, you are aware of the implications?"

***

Thoughts flooded April's mind as she drove along the Harrogate Road towards Pool-in-Wharfdale. For some reason she could not get the image of Patricia and her baby out of her head. It seemed to have been burned there, black and white, the colour of ash. The windscreen wipers protested briefly at the lack of water; the misty drizzle had ceased but the salt-laden spray from the preceding and passing vehicles contrived to turn the windscreen opaque. Relieved, she turned off the main road and washed the screen again.

On this occasion April had not called in advance to make an appointment. Out of instinct she drove around the village taking in most of the road system. There was always a chance the silver Skoda could be parked within the vicinity, after all, she believed a mother's love knew no bounds. Pulling up in the pub car park, she glanced at the large and impressive stone building that seemed to be protected from the road by a collection of outdoor seats and tables. Climbing from the car she checked the few vehicles that were parked. None matched the one for which she searched and within minutes she turned off Green Hill and onto Brackenwell Lane.

On hearing the knock, Lynda Gough looked surprised as she glanced from behind the net curtains covering the front window. Within seconds the door opened.

"Don't stand there like cheese at four pence, come in." The greeting was warm and sincere if a little strange.

"Mrs Gough, I'm sorry to call unannounced but I really need your help with the inquiry."

"Wipe your feet, love, and take a seat. The fire's good. Can I get the tea you didn't have last time?" She grinned. "It's not the same one, I'll have you know."

"Thank you, that would be so kind."

April deliberately went over much of what was said on the previous visit and many of the answers were the same. She felt, however, that Lynda sensed her questions were skirting the real reason she had come.

"What've you actually come for, love?"

"Do you know if Joshua has been working since I last called?"

She frowned. "As far as I know. He never stops, he's like his dad was, has a strong work ethic. Come to think of it, he usually rings me on a Wednesday but he didn't this week. Is he in trouble?"

"We don't believe his car has moved in the last five days. Do you have his mobile number?"

"I do. I rarely call owing to cost as he rings me."

"Will you call him now just for our own peace of mind, please."

Lynda crossed the room, picked up the phone before returning to sit down. "He bought me this so I could take it in the garden." She tapped in a number. April immediately heard the automated voice inform them that the number was no longer available. She also saw the confused look on Lynda's face. She tried again with the same result.

"Is that the only number you have for Joshua?"

"He doesn't have a landline but has a separate mobile for his taxi." She tried that. There was no response. "Now that's strange. His business phone is never off."

"Mrs Gough, we're worried for the wellbeing of your

son."

"Is he in trouble?"

"I can't say. All I can say is we need to find him. Do you know where he might go when he's not at home?"

She shook her head. "I hope he would come here if he needed help."

"His wife?" The words sounded hollow but the possibility was always there.

"She moved south and they never stayed in touch. I wouldn't know where she is."

"I'm going to ask something now that might offend you but for Joshua's sake, for your son's sake, I need the truth." April leaned forward and touched both Lynda's hands. "Is Joshua your son?"

April felt Lynda's hands clench onto her skirt and her whole body stiffen before she saw her head swing slowly from side to side. She released a hand and withdrew a lace handkerchief from beneath her cardigan sleeve.

"He's Patty's lad." She blew her nose and dabbed each cheek.

April watched the tears flow. She had seen enough false tears in the Interview Rooms and in Court to appreciate these were genuine, as if the suppressed secret of the truth had built up over the years behind a wall of guilt that was now beginning to crumble.

"When she told me she was expecting she was heartbroken. She was terrified of what her dad would say and kept it secret as long as she could. Her mum was furious too. She was away at college which meant her mother didn't see the morning sickness but when she knew, she told her she'd ruined her chances of ever becoming a teacher of ever being a success in life. She had brought shame on the whole family through her selfish actions. She was sent away from home, first to a relative and then the home for unmarried mothers."

"Did she keep in touch?"

"She did. I was married to Jimmy and we'd been trying for a child but with no success. He was sick for a lad. We went up to see her, spoke with the person in charge and said we'd like to adopt the child. It meant so much to Patty knowing her baby would be in safe hands and when it was a boy, my Jimmy was over the moon. And that's why she saw him over the years. She really watched him grow up. I thought it only right. Nothing was said to Jo, we'd promised each other. He really had two mums."

April felt a lump grow in her throat.

"But at the beginning, it wasn't as easy as that. When the boy was born Patty called him Fraser. We went up that very day purely by chance. When we got there, we were met by a woman, a Miss Cole, and even though we'd been promised the child she said there'd been a mistake, we could no longer foster and adopt Patty's child. She had another family ready to take him."

"Cole?"

"Betty Cole. I'll never ever forget her and neither did my Jimmy. The way she was going to simply dismiss us, dismiss what Patty wanted. We were left in a state of shock as she left us and went into another room. Jimmy told me to wait and he followed her. He was away a while. I thought he was going to scream and shout but I heard no raised voices. I don't know what he said but after ten minutes he returned with her. She looked proper flushed, anxious but she said that Jimmy had explained the situation and she now realised Patty had promised the child to us and we could take him ... she then stopped conversing. She took us straight to see Patty and the baby. I took the photograph you showed me. We always made copies for Patty."

"Did you ever find out the name of the father?"

"She believed it might be Rodney Crookson, you know the man. Even though after his seduction, she told me she had a few one night stands as if in defiance."

"She could have taken back the child, maybe when she married," April suggested.

"Philip was kind but would not entertain the idea, he didn't want the daily reminder of her promiscuity. Those were his words. He even tried to prevent contact. What we did we did in secret. Philip, as far as I know, never harmed her but he threw up a barrier even though she told me he had promised she could see the child."

"You have twins?"

"They're ours. As soon as we had a baby in the house it must have made me more fertile. I became pregnant straight away. Jimmy said that's what happens with the sheep. He saw it all the time with the animals on the farm. A barren ewe is given a lamb and then left with the tup and ..."

April reflected on the cruelty of the story she had witnessed and on the occasions the word 'promised' came up she could not fail to visualise the victims.

"Do you have anything here that still belongs to Joshua? We need to check his DNA. I hope we will not need it."

Lynda moved from the room returning with a flat cap. "He wears this when he's here. You'll bring it back?"

Chapter 28

The late briefing was organised quickly as the day was coming to a close. Everyone was ready for home. Cyril was tired but knew the investigation was beginning to come together as more evidence was gathered. He was still expecting a few curved balls to land at his feet. He regarded each team member before consulting his notes.

"We have a positive profile. Joshua is Patricia Melling's son but we also have confirmation from the DNA tests that Crookson was not the father. There's confirmation Joshua was at the scene of all three murders, and that he was present over a number of visits at Spencer's house. We can presume the raised voices heard by Spencer's neighbours may well have been Joshua and Spencer. April."

April stood and explained in greater detail the evidence she had received from Lynda Gough. "Lynda also believed her husband told Joshua the full story when he knew he was dying. Until that time, he believed he was their child and Auntie Pat was just that. Jim Gough always believed Joshua's father was Crookson."

"So, who was the child who played with Joshua when they met in the park?"

"As you know she did some child care, voluntary work, and he was one of the children. They formed a firm friendship. All we have to do now is find Joshua."

"I can, from what we've heard from Lynda, see the possible reason to seek revenge on Cole and Spencer but I fail to link anything to Meredith."

"We may only know that if and when we find Joshua. I cannot at this stage comprehend his mental state."

"We've put out a public call for information regarding Joshua Gough and the car registration. It's on all the socials."

***

Cyril Bennett was walking home when the call came through from one of the team who had just started their shift.

"We have in the last ten minutes received a report of a body found. Male. From the photograph we hold, it's been confirmed as Gough."

"Where?" Cyril paused, focused on the many tail lights that streamed like red fire flies down Otley Road.

"Washed into the banking in the River Swale, Richmond. First responders are there. Found by a dog walker. They've also located the car."

"Like the salmon, they return to the place of their birth," Cyril announced, unintentionally voicing his thoughts.

"Sorry?"

"Never mind. Please go on."

"As I said, we've found his car too. Skoda, silver but he'd changed the lettering on the plates with a felt pen can you believe! On the passenger seat was a pack of cards. Two were left on the dashboard, the ace of hearts and ace of clubs." The caller paused allowing Cyril to understand the possible significance.

"I thought the ace of spades was the symbol of death?"

"Clubs, if you've used a bottle to …"

"Indeed. How foolish of me."

"We found his phone inside the car and a photograph of him with his adoptive parents. The phone's with Digital Forensics with an urgent request. They're looking for photographs and any voice notes."

"Keep me informed if you have any further news." Cyril paused. The first line of a Philip Larkin poem came to mind. *They fuck you up, your mum and dad.*' He thought for a moment on his own upbringing. *'And don't have any kids yourself.*' He reflected on the fact that none of the victims had children themselves.

***

The photographs retrieved of the Richmond crime scene had been added to the board as the team listened to the saved voice note secured from Gough's phone.

"This may be a ramble but it has to be said as I will not be here to tell the tale and I don't want you to waste your valuable time looking for ghosts. When Dad told me the truth I was really confused and traumatised. I know I'm no kid, no innocent child but I've cried like a baby, my world is upside down and inside out. How could people who have always loved me, hide the truth from me for nearly a lifetime? I know they concealed the truth through genuine, deep love, love not just for me but also for Auntie Pat. It was to protect me and because they'd made a promise to Auntie Pat … But it still hurts, it still cuts like a knife when I think about it and I think about it more and more. Weren't they wrong? I know they tried to keep their promise but what promise should keep a child from loving its real mother?"

The trembling and uncertainty in Gough's voice was pitiful. The sobs were clear as were the inaudible mutterings as if he were arguing and fighting with himself. There was a long pause before he spoke again

"When I knew everything, I made a promise at my dad's grave that the people who I discovered to be involved, people who broke promises or hurt Auntie Pat should suffer. And I kept that promise, an oath I had made from the time I discovered the truth. My mother, Lynda, who to me had always been my real mother, taught me the story of Joshua, how he led his people to the promised land. Dad told me what Cole tried to do, to give me to another family after I had been promised to them. She promised for fuck's sake. Fucking promised!" His anger was evident. "He told me he'd informed Cole that her promise meant nothing and if they did not adopt me, then he would ensure she would, at some time in the future, go missing never to be found. He knew from that moment she would be constantly worrying about when the hammer would fall. I know he could have said that to her, threaten her to change her mind. Dad always had a very persuasive way. I'd seen him deal with poachers and the like. As for Spencer, I hated him. He once found mum and me with Auntie Pat and he lost his temper. I could see real fear in Auntie Pat's eyes. She deserved better than him.

"When I knew the whole truth, she had sadly passed away. I went with mum to see her in hospital, to say goodbye but even then, she was still Auntie Pat. I had no idea. Dad came too, so we knew Spencer would say nothing if he saw us. I tried to talk to Spencer a few times but he just started shouting. He wouldn't listen. I tried to forgive him. In the end I enjoyed killing him. When he saw me that night, he showed the same fear as Auntie Pat had done that day. When he found us all together. It was only a moment but it was in his eyes and that made it so worthwhile. You'll be wondering about Meredith."

Cyril paused the recording. "It's clear he's been drinking heavily." They had all heard a definite slurring in his speech.

"That was fate, just a chance meeting. He'd booked a taxi on occasion. It's amazing what people talk about when they're in the back. 'Have you been busy' or 'Are you finishing soon' but not him. He was a little tipsy, told me he'd been a caretaker of a children's home. He then mentioned Betty Cole, they were friends and he asked if I knew her, and if I knew she was a Harrogate celebrity, that she'd been given an MBE? I realised I'd picked him up at her house and I'd dropped him at her house on two other occasions. He also told me he'd fought in the Falklands War; every time he told me he'd fought in the bloody Falklands. Dad had mentioned Cole and he spit when he said her name and then it all fit into place, like when patience comes out after a few games of trying."

There was a long pause but the background sounds were still audible. It was as if he were pausing to take a further drink.

"If I'd known of any others who'd worked at the home, I'd have killed them too. I could have killed Crookson, not for what he did, but for what he didn't do. He should have looked after Auntie Pat properly. I gave him an envelope. I wanted him to think about what he'd done, for him to understand that he, as much as me, is responsible for the deaths. Without him, none of this would have happened. I could have killed him but he was, after all, my real father. I could've just strangled him that night but I wanted him to suffer like mum and me the bast ..."

The ending of the recording was abrupt. People in the room remained silent trying to comprehend the logic but Cyril didn't miss the irony of the interrupted final word.

"And he loved Lynda? What will she do when she hears?" Shakti's facial expression spoke a thousand words.

Owen broke the short silence. "What about Mary Bailey burning what we believed to be historical evidence?"

April responded. "She was questioned and had no idea of the significance of the documentation. As she said, a lady of Betty's age stored boxes of material, much of which was out of date and a good deal of which had no relevance or value to her. She didn't seem shocked to hear of Crookson's admission, after all, she'd witnessed his behaviour. Cole, knowing Mary was with him that day, probably had a bearing on his behaviour to a degree and she remained safe! They're now just hoping to put everything behind them and head back home to France as soon as possible but these things take time and I can't see the estate being released for quite a while."

Cyril collected the sheets of paper before him. He could

still hear Gough's words tumbling in his head, the words of a forgotten and emotionally abused child. One cruel act had festered within him, creating insecurity and doubt. Cyril's thought process eventually came full circle, *Gough resembled the wild salmon returning to die at its place of birth.*

Chapter 29

Cyril stood and watched the whiteboard slowly being stripped of the details. He held onto the photograph of Patricia Melling holding her newborn. *Who'd have thought that the birth of one child would eventually result in the deaths of three people who, in a strange way, believed they were being altruistic, doing the right things in life.*

He also collected the yin and yang symbol and walked through to his office before dropping both the photograph and drawing onto his desk. He sighed and looked across towards the framed photograph of Liz. "As long as I'm in this job, Liz, I don't think I'll ever fully understand the complexities of the human mind."

Liz had been killed in a revenge kidnap by a man Cyril had arrested earlier in his career; the guilt had remained with him and nearly destroyed him. In some ways and in retrospect, he believed he could identify with Gough's anger and frustration.

"Uncle Cyril!" The voice of Christopher and the sound of his running feet made Cyril turn. Dressed still as Spiderman, he held out a finger and made a strange sound. Owen followed.

"Be careful! He'll trap you in his web."

Cyril collected the child and flew him in a wide circle before popping him down.

"We've come to show you something."

Christopher clung onto Cyril's leg as Owen removed what appeared to be a photograph from his pocket. "I know you're probably sick to death of photographs but we thought you'd like to be the first person to see this one."

Cyril took the photograph. It was a 3-D ultrasound image.

"I'm going to be a father again. That's at ten weeks, sir. You and Julie are the first to know. Spiderman here's seen it but unfortunately, he's not too impressed as he can't see any muscles or a cape!"

Cyril laughed as he bent and kissed the boy on the forehead. Picking up the photograph of Patricia and the yin and yang symbol, he held both in his hands. "I think I now understand the meaning of why that symbol meant so much to Gough, a boy confused. The light and the dark, the good and the bad."

"Really, sir?"

"Maybe I'm seeing things that aren't there, maybe Gough knew more than his parents would have ever anticipated. Possibly a natural understanding." He stuck out a hand and took Owen's. "I couldn't be happier for you and your family."

"Thank you, that means a great deal to me. You've been like a father to me and I want you to know that I'm truly grateful."

Cyril patted his arm.

"Hannah and I would like you and Julie to pop round for

a glass of something special later this evening."

"I'd like that, Owen, we'd like that. Thank you and I'm thrilled for you all. Family life is just so important." As Owen left, he could hear Christopher's laughter fade away. He looked down at the photograph of a lost mother and child. He closed his eyes and whispered, "Rest in peace, Joshua, rest in peace."

Featured Artist

It is wonderful that I receive so much feedback on this element of the Harrogate Crime Series. It is an element about which I love to write as it means I am bringing some of my favourite northern artists to the fore. I do try to own or have owned the artists mentioned but I can also dream. You will, I feel, have guessed the artist.

Reginald Grange Brundrit
Royal Academician.
1883 – 1960

I have more than a link with this artist as Reginald Brundrit was born in Liverpool, the setting for my other crime series. He moved in his youth to Bradford, the place of my birth. He was educated at Bradford Grammar and then studied painting at Bradford School of Art, the Slade, and privately with John M Swan in Kensington.

An artist who forged a successful career as a portrait and landscape artist in London, he moved north to settle in Linton, near Grassington. He was known for his idyllic north-country landscapes, many painted in the Yorkshire

Dales. During the First World War, he served in the Armed Forces, later moving to Masham, Black Sheep Ale country!

Studying carefully a large selection of his paintings, there is a clear mix of styles from the loose and expressionistic to the fine detailed oils set within the Wharf Valley. However, each painting captures the wonder and beauty of Yorkshire wearing her many seasonal masks. His depiction of 'The River' (Held by Bradford Museums and Galleries) is in direct contrast to the wonderful painting 'Veiled Morning'.

Surprisingly, his paintings do come up for auction frequently and it will only be a matter of time before I find the one I would like.

Acknowledgements

The poems used with thanks:

'The Highwayman'
'The moon was a ghostly galleon tossed upon cloudy seas,'
Alfred Noyes.
(1880 – 1958)

'This be the Verse'
Philip Larkin.
(1922 – 1985)

I have thoroughly enjoyed popping back over the Pennines to Harrogate to write book fourteen of the Harrogate Crime Series, to be reacquainted with DCI Cyril Bennett and his team. Strangely enough, it doesn't seem nine years ago since these characters were but ideas in my head, wondering if I would ever write the first book at all. And here we are, book fourteen finished as well as three books set over in Merseyside.

They say that everyone has a book inside them but I must have been a little greedy as I have eighteen published as well as a number of short stories. It is you, dear reader I have to thank for the support and encouragement I receive to write another. Bless you!

Writing is a solitary business, it's a time when I'm wrapped in a parallel world, a world filled with murder. My wife believes my personality and character changes when I write but I suppose when you are mentally juggling scenes and speaking in the tongues of a number of characters, it will have a bearing! To Debbie, who puts up with a great deal of the writer's angst, my love and sincere thanks.

Accuracy is key and I do thank those who wish to remain anonymous for their valuable contribution to this book. I can, however, name a few. To Jane Clark and Professor Kenton Morgan for their help in discovering more about horse serum, a fascinating subject as my late brother suffered a serious reaction to the vaccine when he was a child.

I try to make the places, the streets and the buildings as accurate as possible and how fortunate that real roadworks were taking place at Kex Gill at the time of writing. The closure of the main A59 was in some ways the inspiration for part of the story. However, creative licence has played a part. The mother and baby home set in Richmond is fictitious, I felt the subject too upsetting and delicate to use a true setting. The Stray still features heavily and is magnificent in all weathers and all seasons.

To the social media book groups, I would like to offer my sincere thanks for your continued support. To Lynda Checkley (Here she is in real life), Sam Brownley, Dee Groocock, Donna Morfett (Now an author in her own right), Sarah Hardy, Livia Sbarbaro, Caroline Vincent (Cole), Donna Wilbor, Beyond the Books, Deb Day, Peter Fleming,

Michelle Ryles, Sue Burns, Andrew Forsyth, Geoff Blakesley and Susan Hunter. I'm sure to have missed some people and if I have, my apologies and thank you.

To Helen Gray and Ian Cleverdon who cast their keen eyes on each and every word.

To Craig Benyon at Create Print for your support with the cover design.

A huge thank you to 'Paper, People, Books', a new independent book shop in Pateley Bridge for kindly stocking the whole series and 'The Little Ripon Bookshop'. Independent bookshops play a key role in helping both published and self-published authors reach a wider audience. Your support means a great deal.

Finally, to close, it is to you holding the book or the Kindle, the reader, to whom I offer my sincere thanks. Without you there would be little point in continuing with the series. It is gratifying to see that not only readers from the UK but also from around the world are finding DCI Cyril Bennett and his team. It is an honour to introduce to you the wonderful spa town of Harrogate and the magnificent Yorkshire Dales.

If you have enjoyed this book or the series then please tell your family and friends as word of mouth is the best way to bring more readers to the series.

Until the next time.

Thank you and best wishes,

Malcolm

www.malcolmhollingdrakeauthor.co.uk

Malcolm Hollingdrake

Printed in Great Britain
by Amazon